Abigail
Iris

THE PET
PROJECT

Also by Lisa Glatt, Suzanne Greenberg, and
Joy Allen

Abigail Iris: The One and Only

Abigail Iris

THE PET PROJECT

Lisa Glatt and
Suzanne Greenberg

illustrated by Joy Allen

Walker & Company ✸ New York

Text copyright © 2010 by Lisa Glatt and Suzanne Greenberg
Illustrations copyright © 2010 by Joy Allen

All rights reserved. No part of this book may be reproduced or transmitted in any form or by
any means, electronic or mechanical, including photocopying, recording, or by any information
storage and retrieval system, without permission in writing from the publisher.

First published in the United States of America in March 2010
by Walker Publishing Company, Inc., a division of Bloomsbury Publishing, Inc.
Paperback edition published in April 2011
www.bloomsburykids.com

For information about permission to reproduce selections from this book, write to
Permissions, Walker BFYR, 175 Fifth Avenue, New York, New York 10010

The Library of Congress has cataloged the hardcover edition as follows:
Glatt, Lisa.
Abigail Iris : the pet project / by Lisa Glatt and Suzanne Greenberg ; illustrated by Joy Allen.
p.   cm.
Summary: When Abigail Iris finally gets the new kitten she has been
wanting, she learns about the responsibilities that come with pet ownership,
as well as the impact a kitten can have on a large family like hers.
ISBN 978-0-8027-8657-9 (hardcover)
[1. Cats—Fiction. 2. Animals—Infancy—Fiction. 3. Family life—California—Fiction.
4. Brothers and sisters—Fiction. 5. Allergy—Fiction. 6. California—Fiction.]
I. Greenberg, Suzanne. II. Allen, Joy, ill. III. Title.
PZ7.G48143735Abf 2010   [Fic]—dc22   2009019197

ISBN 978-0-8027-2235-5 (paperback)

Book design by Yelena Safronova
Printed in the U.S.A. by Quad/Graphics, Fairfield, Pennsylvania
2 4 6 8 10 9 7 5 3 1

All papers used by Bloomsbury Publishing, Inc., are natural, recyclable products
made from wood grown in well-managed forests. The manufacturing processes
conform to the environmental regulations of the country of origin.

For Scarlet Liang —L. G.

To Joel, Claire, and Noah, and in memory of
Ginger and Annie, family —S. G.

To my spunky and fun "Mom" —J. A.

Abigail Iris

THE PET PROJECT

Chapter 1

"The Onlies don't just get birthdays, they get half birthdays, too," I tell my mother.

"Oh, Abigail Iris. Who ever heard of such a thing? Do they get half a cake, half a present? Even you have to think that's a bit silly."

"No, I don't," I say, but my mother is already moving on to the next vegetable stand, eyeing a big heap of tiny blue potatoes. "I don't think it's silly at all," I say just in case she wasn't fully listening.

"Do they have quarter birthdays, too?" my mother says.

"That would be silly, Mom," I say. "I'm being serious."

The Onlies are my three best friends: Cynthia, Rebecca, and Genevieve. They're lucky enough to be only children and have half birthdays in addition to whole ones, but my mother points out regularly that I'm lucky too, because I have a nice family, and, in her opinion, a particularly delightful mother.

"Will you just look at those?" she says about the blue potatoes, but I can tell she's talking more to herself than to me. No one can get more excited about vegetables than my mother. I look around for a sample, but then I remember that people don't eat raw potatoes even if they are a very pretty blue.

The best thing about the farmers' market on Sunday mornings is the samples. The second best thing is having my mother to myself since Victoria prefers to spend Sunday mornings in our bedroom with the door shut and me out of our room while she does her middle school homework. And my brothers never want to go even if there are so many free samples of different kinds of strawberries you can turn your fingers bright red trying them all.

The farmers' market is just a bunch of stands set up in a row in the marina parking lot, but it doesn't feel like a parking lot anymore when the farmers are there. It feels more like a little tiny part of the Orange County fair where everyone shows off the vegetables they grew themselves. My mother says it's important to support local farmers. She explains this idea to me every Sunday while we are driving over. I nod seriously when she talks even though I'm mostly thinking about whether I'm going to get kettle corn or cheese popcorn from the popcorn man.

Once, my mother got so excited about vegetables before I was born that she tried to grow a garden of our own in the backyard, but she said it was just too shady out there and nothing got big enough.

The old Fuji apple man with the wire glasses and bald spot on the top of his head is handing out apple slices. I say, "Yes, please,"

and take one even though I already know what a Fuji apple tastes like because I sample this particular kind of apple every week from the apple man. He winks at me and gives me a second sample.

"Sweet as candy," he says to a lady walking by in a big hurry, which is not the way to walk through the farmers' market, in my opinion.

I can see the blue potatoes right through the clear plastic bag in the basket my mother's holding when she walks up and samples an apple. "I just couldn't resist," she says. "Blue potatoes. What do you think they taste like? They look too pretty to cook."

"They do," I say.

"Oh, let's get some of the Fuji apples, too."

This is the good thing about my mother. She may be a grown-up and a teacher and we may be on a budget, but sometimes she just can't resist things.

We are almost at the end of the market where the cat-rescue people always set up on

Sunday, and I hope she's in the mood not to resist some more.

"I think a pet would make a very appropriate half-birthday present," I say to my mother. We pull our bags up our arms a little so we can hold hands, and I lead her past the flower stands to the cats. They are my number three favorite thing about the farmers' market. They are already above the popcorn I always get when we're done shopping, and they would move right up to number one, past the samples, if I ever got to take a kitten home.

"A pet is a very big responsibility, Abigail Iris," she says. "We can look, but half birthday or not, you know we can't bring a cat home. We've been over this before."

"I know," I say, but I don't know for sure.

We always hold the rescued cats when we're ready to take a break from our shopping, even though it makes us both sad to say good-bye to them. My mother says it's very relaxing to hold a cat. When she married my dad, he had two little boys already—my brothers—and my parents decided to have Victoria and me instead of a pet. That's what she always tells me when I get into my why-can't-we-have-a-cat mood.

"My mother would like to hold the big fat gray one," I say to the cat-rescue lady in charge today, picking out the fattest, laziest-looking cat. The cat lady puts down the book she's reading and reaches into a cage and hands my mother the cat I picked for her.

My mother sits on the folding chair with the cat in her lap and lets out a deep sigh. "So pretty," she says. "You're a pretty boy, aren't you?"

Now that my mother is all set up, I peek in another cage. All I see in there is a big stuffed teddy bear, and I'm thinking the cat-rescue lady might need to wear better glasses when she goes out to do her rescuing.

"He likes to hide behind it, especially when he's sleeping," she says.

And then I see what she's talking about, two white paws and a little black tail curled up around the back side of the teddy bear.

"He's about three months old, we think,"
the cat lady says to me. "Someone found him
in the Albertson's parking lot behind the trash
bin. Isn't he cute?"

I peek behind the teddy bear and see him,
a black kitty. *Of course he's cute*, I'm thinking. *Is
there anything cuter?* But I don't say a word
because sometimes it's better
to play it cool when you
really want something,
as my brother
Eddie always
tells me. He's a
teenager, and
although I don't
prefer to admit
it, he knows
more things
about the world
than I do.

"It's my half
birthday next
week," I say to

ADOPT TODAY

the cat lady. "I'm thinking about getting a kitten this year."

"Is that right?" she says. The cat lady raises one eyebrow at me, which is something I wish I knew how to do with my face. My Only friend Cynthia knows how to wiggle her ears without touching them, and my brother Cameron can burp "My Country 'Tis of Thee" after he drinks a can of Sprite, but I don't have one single trick.

"Can I hold him?" I ask.

"Well, I don't know," she says, smiling. "You have to be very gentle."

"Of course," I say.

"He can be pretty wriggly," she says.

"I'm a good holder," I say.

She reaches in and picks up the kitten for me. I see a bright orange spot on his nose, and I think right away that this kitten must be named Spot even though it's a dog's name, and I hope he won't mind. She hands him to me, and I try my hardest to hold Spot gently without letting him wiggle out of my arms. He crawls up on my chest and buries his nose with the orange spot on it into my neck, and then he's very still, and I can feel his heart beating.

"I think he's scared," I say.

"He likes you," the cat lady says. "See, he's not even trying to get away."

My mother is handing the fat gray cat back to the cat lady and telling me it's time to go. "What a baby," she says about my kitten.

"Can we keep him, Mom, please, please, please?" I say, not being cool at all now. "A kitten is like half a cat and that would be the present I would most prefer in the whole world for my half birthday."

"He's very sweet," my mother says.

I'm waiting for her to say *but*, but I don't hear it right away, so I speak quickly before she can get it out. "He likes me," I say. "He's not even trying to get away. I would take care of him. I would feed him and change his litter box and buy him little toys with my allowance."

"Is that right?" my mother says.

The cat lady is giving her a business card

with her phone number on it. "You two need to think about this," she says. "A pet is a big responsibility. It's nothing to take lightly."

Whose side are you on, cat-rescue lady? I'm thinking, but my mother is putting the card in a special zippered compartment inside her purse, not just stuffing it into her pants pocket, so this went better than it might have.

"Maybe we'll bring up the idea to your dad tonight," she says to me as we pick up our bags and walk back toward the popcorn man. "See what he thinks about a cat now that you all are older. Maybe it's time."

"You are the best, best mother," I say.

"Now, Abigail Iris, don't get your hopes up," she says.

"I won't," I say, but of course I do.

My mother waits in the popcorn line with me, and I'm so excited I forget to pick my flavor until I'm right at the front of the line, and it's my turn to order. I sample the cheesy and the kettle corn and then I sample the cheesy again, Victoria's favorite, and my mother says,

"Abigail Iris, people are waiting. Just give her a bag of each."

I am so happy thinking about Spot that I promise to share my popcorn when we get home. I am so happy that, instead of taking second samples on all the strawberries I can find, I help my mother pick out green beans she plans to make for dinner in case the blue potatoes are not a complete hit.

Chapter 2

Second Street is the best street in Long Beach, in my opinion. It is the street I prefer and the one that my three best friends prefer too. Sometimes there is traffic on Second Street, and yes, there is another, quieter way to get to our house, but today my mom prefers Second Street too, so we agree to take it home. My mom says that Second Street is full of life and that sometimes even when you're just driving by, it's good to look out your car window and absorb some of the happy activity going on.

There are shoe stores and ice-cream shops and children's clothing stores, one of which is my favorite. There are also restaurants, *cafes*, my mom calls them, with little tables and chairs on the sidewalk. People are sitting there talking and eating and drinking coffee. If I were sitting at a little table talking to people, I would be drinking hot chocolate, which is what I prefer.

There's an old man who walks down Second Street with a parrot on his shoulder. Sometimes, if you're lucky enough to be walking down the street the opposite way he's walking, the parrot will talk to you. He says things like "hello" and "good morning" and "nice day, isn't it?" which is very impressive, if you ask me. People walk their dogs on Second Street too, and when we're waiting at a stop sign, I see one of my Only best friends, Rebecca, with her father and their dog, Jazzy. I am hanging out the window, so excited, waving and waving, until Rebecca sees me and comes walking up to my mom's car. Rebecca's usually my silly Only friend, but these days, she's more serious. Her dad stands back with

Jazzy, who is doing his business on the lawn, which would be, of course, not my favorite thing about adopting a pet, but a girl must do what she must do, is what I'm thinking.

"We were at the farmers' market," I tell Rebecca. "We got popcorn and green beans and blue potatoes—oh, and we might adopt a kitten for my half birthday."

"Don't get ahead of yourself, Abigail Iris," my mom says. She smiles at Rebecca and says hello.

"How exciting, a kitten," Rebecca says. Behind her, Jazzy is still doing his business, and Rebecca's dad is waving at us.

"How's your mom doing?" my mom asks, because Rebecca's mom is pregnant, which means that Rebecca's time as an Only is very limited. I've told her more than once to enjoy it while she can.

"We can't eat anything spicy, and her feet are too fat for her shoes, but she's the same mostly, I guess," Rebecca says.

When Rebecca's dad is finished crouching

over Jazzy's business with his plastic bag, he drops it in the trash and walks up to the sidewalk too.

"Hi, Henry," my mom says, leaning over me. "Rebecca says Martha's doing okay."

"She's fine, a real champ." Rebecca's dad is smiling. His cheeks are red from the sun and his hair is gray on the sides.

When a car pulls up behind us and honks, we know it is our time to move along, so my mom says, "Send Martha our best wishes," and then we drive away. When I see Jazzy's twitching tail, I am reminded, of course, of how petless I, Abigail Iris, really am, and that what I need and want for my very important half birthday is for Spot to come and live with me.

Still, the rest of the way home, I am trying not to bug my mom by talking about Spot the whole time, but apparently I am talking about Spot the whole time because when we stop at a red light on Argonne Street, she says, "Enough's enough, Abigail Iris."

"Okay," I say, "then let's talk about my half birthday."

"Isn't that really just talking about Spot?" She looks at me and sighs and the light turns green, so I say what I've heard my dad say, which is, "How green is green enough?" but I say it with a smile.

My mom moves her foot from the brake to the gas pedal and we lurch forward a little bit. "I shouldn't have let you name him," she says, under her breath. "When we get home, let me talk to your dad first. And don't tell him that you named him. Don't call him Spot, okay? Call him 'the kitten,'" she says.

I don't know why she says this, but my mother is very smart and I can tell that she's thinking hard about things. Still, I get the feeling that she's on my side, even if she told me "enough's enough."

"You know what's best," I say, and it feels like we're in cahoots and that maybe she's thinking about Spot as much as I am.

"He sure was cute," she says. "I must admit."

"I thought we weren't going to talk about Spot," I tell her.

"The kitten," she corrects me.

"The kitten," I say. "The kitten, the kitten, the kitten."

"Good girl," she says, smiling.

※

When we get home my dad is outside in his robe, watering the lawn. I carry the bag with the blue potatoes and I am very proud of them when I show the bag to my dad. I reach inside and pick out the bluest potato I can find and hand it to him. "We're having blue mashed potatoes tonight, Old Man Cheeto." This is my dad's nickname because he's a snacker.

"Very good," he says.

"When you're done watering, I need to talk to you," my mom says.

"Oh no," my dad says, joking. "What did I do now?"

My mom pats him on the shoulder and assures him that he's a very good husband and a very good dad, and then he turns off the hose, wraps it up into its nice little coil, and follows us inside.

In the kitchen, my dad takes our bags and sets them on the counter. I'm sitting on a stool helping unpack, and everyone is surprised, even my mom and me who picked everything out, by how bright and beautiful and fresh it all is. There are green beans, and red and yellow peppers; there's an onion nearly as big as a tetherball; there are peanuts in their shell, corn on the cob still wrapped up in their little straw coats, the two bags of delicious popcorn, and of course, of course, those blue potatoes.

"We saw Henry and Rebecca on Second Street," my mom tells my dad.

"And Jazzy too," I say.

"How's Martha doing?" he wants to know.

"Just the usual complaints," my mom says.

Victoria is on the phone like she's always on the phone these days, and when she turns the corner and steps into the kitchen, she sees that we're home, looks Mom in the eye, and then quickly says, "See you later" and turns off her cell phone. "Can I go to Carla's for dinner tonight?" she asks my mom.

"Tonight's family night," my mom says.

Victoria groans like family night is a trip to the dentist, and my mom kisses her on the top of her head and says, "You can peel the potatoes later with Abigail Iris."

"Oh great," Victoria says, all sarcastic, but I can tell she sort of wants to do it.

Later on, while my sister and I are alone in the kitchen eating cheesy popcorn, my mom and dad are in the living room on the couch, having a talk, hopefully about Spot. My sister and I are taking a break from peeling potatoes. I'm sitting at the table and Victoria is leaning against the sink. The popcorn is between us and we take turns dipping our hands into the bag. In between bites, I look at my sister for too long until she says, "What, Abigail Iris? Spit it out."

And I can't hold it in any longer, so I blurt,

"I think mom's going to get me a kitten for my half birthday."

"Half birthday? What is that?" she says, plucking one kernel at a time from her open palm and putting it daintily in her mouth. That is *not* how I eat popcorn at all. I'm a handful sort of person, which is what my dad told me at the movies once. "*You go for the gusto,*" is what he said. Although I had no idea what that meant and couldn't ask him because the movie was about to start, I did get my definition from him later. Going for the gusto meant I was a very enthusiastic sort of person.

"I'll be eight and a half next week," I remind her. "Do you not remember my half birthday?"

Victoria rolls her eyes and then it occurs to her what I really just said. "A cat? A real live kitty-cat?" And she's smiling and happy too, but I know nothing is a sure thing yet, so I say, "Maybe," and then I stress the word, sounding just like my mom. "Just *maybe*, Victoria. Let's just wait and see."

Chapter 3

My brother Cameron says that the blue mashed potatoes look like they're filled with mold and almost ruins everyone's appetite.

"Blue cheese *is* actually filled with mold," Eddie says, very proud, as always, of his advanced high school science skills.

"How interesting," my father, Old Man Cheeto, says.

"Maybe I should have broiled the potatoes," my mother says.

"And yogurt's alive," Eddie says. "It's made with bacteria. They add it to the milk."

"Or sauteed them," my mother says, still talking about the potatoes.

"Could you please stop explaining everything, Eddie?" Victoria says, putting her spoon full of blue mashed potatoes down on her plate. She is already the most picky eater of all of us and clearly doesn't need any more interesting food news.

"Dead or alive, I am not a fan of yogurt," I announce in case anyone is unaware of this fact. "Unless it's the frozen kind you can request sprinkles on top of. On a cone," I add, so my mother doesn't misunderstand and try to pack me regular yogurt for lunch.

The cone makes me think about how sometimes Rebecca's dad buys their dog, Jazzy, an ice-cream cone—plain vanilla only because of his delicate digestion—when he buys us one on Second Street in the summer, and I wonder if it's time to bring up my kitten.

I clear my throat and shoot my mom a look, and she shrugs her shoulders, which is something not at all like her to do. I am wishing we could go into another room for a little talk first, but Cameron is already asking me what all the faces are about. The dinner table is the place where all urgent points of the day are discussed, and he can see I'm getting ready to say something important.

"Cough it up, Abigail Iris," Cameron says, reaching for seconds from the bowl of blue mashed potatoes, which he seems very fond of even if he does think they look like they're filled with mold.

"I have an announcement to make," I say. "We have decided to adopt a kitten for my half birthday next week."

"Your what?" Cameron says.

"We have?" Eddie says.

"His name is Spot," I say, remembering too late about how I'm not supposed to bring up the fact of his name yet.

"Now, Abigail Iris," my father says. "Don't jump ahead. We're in the discussion stage still."

"We are?" I say, very excited because I didn't know my mother had even gotten this far without me for backup. "It's all I want for my half birthday. I won't ask for anything else. I promise."

"Let's not forget someone's full birthday is coming up," my father says, talking about his own, which, in the excitement about the kitten, I had nearly forgot. I realize, doing the subtraction math, it's three days before my half. "We can have a double celebration," I practically shout.

"I'm in favor of the kitten in case anyone cares to know my opinion around here," Victoria says.

"Cats are much easier to take care of than dogs," I tell my father, thinking about Rebecca's dad picking up after Jazzy on Second Street. "For one thing, they use kitty litter."

"Who said anything about a dog?" my father says.

"I'm just making a point," I say.

"Fish are even easier," Victoria says.

I give her a look.

"*I'm* just making a point," she says. "Now can I be excused please to study for my math test?"

After dinner, I sit on Old Man Cheeto's lap in the cushy chair in the living room, and we read our books together. Eddie and Cameron have gone home to their other house, where they live half the time with Kathy and Max and where they have a very old dog named Bruno, who wags his tail when you come in the door but doesn't get up anymore to say

hello. My father used to be married to Kathy before I was born, back in the Stone Age, he always says.

Victoria is upstairs studying her math problems, and my mother is grading papers in the kitchen. Even though it is very quiet, and I have no good excuses to make tomorrow if I'm called on in class to answer a question, I'm too distracted by my new kitten to concentrate on the words of my required book.

"Maybe, Abigail Iris," Old Man Cheeto says to me as if he's reading my mind, which is one of the very special things about my father.

I pretend to be very mature and not nearly as overly excited as I presently feel. "Just wait until you see our kitten," I say. "He can be half your birthday present, too."

"Maybe. Not yes," Old Man Cheeto says. "There's a difference. Your mother and I are still discussing it."

"Of course," I say. I hug Old Man Cheeto very hard and stay quiet, although I would much prefer to ask him a thousand questions like "What's there to discuss?" and "Can we go pick up Spot right this very instant?"

⁓

At lunch the next day at school, I can no longer hold back, and I am so busy telling my three Only best friends—Genevieve, Rebecca, and Cynthia—about Spot that I squeeze my sandwich

too hard and grape jelly spills out all over my white school shirt.

When I run out of everyone's clean napkins to wipe with, I try using the plain side of my sandwich as a napkin, but I just smear the jelly more.

"Put on your jacket," Cynthia says. "If you zip it up, no one will know." Cynthia has had several of

these kinds of run-ins with food herself, and she is the definite expert.

"Your mom will have to use bleach," Rebecca says. "My mom used to bleach all of my school shirts, but she doesn't anymore because of the baby. The baby doesn't like the chemicals."

"But it's not even born yet," Genevieve says. She has her raspberries lined up on her napkin, which she didn't offer up during my spill because it was occupied, and she is eating them one at a time the way she always does. I sneak one and let it sit on my tongue for a minute before I squish it.

"I know," Rebecca says, "and it's already taking over. Did you hear about the party?"

"It's having a party?" Genevieve says. "We need to make a complaint about this to someone." Genevieve's parents are lawyers, and she always has good ideas for complaining.

"It's called a shower," Rebecca says. "The baby gets presents and it's not even here yet to open them."

Secretly I am just a little bit pleased that one of my three Only friends will be an Only no more and will understand some of the problems I have to put up with. Also, I'm thinking there are parts of not being an Only that aren't so bad. For example, a brother or sister can help you argue for what you want, like a kitten. Also, I'm thinking that a little baby might be almost as cute as my kitten, Spot, but I just nod and don't smile when Cynthia says, "Poor you."

※

In my classroom after lunch, I am very warm with my school jacket zipped up to my neck. I unzip it just a little, and then I unzip it the rest of the way, and then I take it off and knock my pencil case off my desk with my elbow. "Everything okay over there, Abigail Iris?" Mrs. Aaronson asks me.

"Just a little warm," I say, picking up my pencils before they roll away. I hold up my geography book to cover my grape-jelly stain, and then Mrs. Aaronson continues her important discussion about our fifty states.

Billy Doil is poking me in the back with a pencil while Mrs. Aaronson talks, and I try hard not to turn around, but I finally have to when I think he's making a pencil mark back there, and I already have enough problems with my grape-jelly stain.

"You missed one," he whispers to me, handing me a pencil.

"Thank you," I say louder than I mean to.

"Five minutes, Abigail Iris," Mrs. Aaronson says.

This means I have to stay after school to practice not interrupting important lessons, and I am not pleased at all with Billy Doil for getting me in trouble.

Genevieve waves a small good-bye to me when the bell rings and she gets to walk outside to freedom, and I sit at my desk very quiet while Mrs. Aaronson tidies up our classroom and puts papers into her book bag to take home.

"How's your sister doing in middle school?" she asks me. Victoria had Mrs. Aaronson for Grade 3 too, but my sister is a perfect student, and I'm sure she never had to stay after school for five minutes. I wonder if this question is a trick to get me to talk, but I decide that even though Mrs. Aaronson may be strict sometimes, she's not a trickster.

"She has homework on the weekends," I say. "It's horrible."

"It's another world, middle school," my teacher says.

"We're thinking about getting a cat," I tell Mrs. Aaronson now that we have clearly broken the quiet-for-five-minutes rule. It is almost okay to stay after school for five minutes alone with Mrs. Aaronson, I am thinking, although I still much prefer to get out with everyone else. "His name is Spot, and my mother and I were introduced to him this weekend at the farmers' market."

"How lovely for you and your family," she says. "Okay, Abigail Iris. Time to pack it up.

Now remember, tomorrow, don't let Billy Doil or anyone else distract you from your work."

"I'll remember," I say, and I give my teacher a very serious face.

"And by the way, you might want to try vinegar on that grape-jelly stain," Mrs. Aaronson adds. We're both done with school for the day, so we walk out of the classroom together and she shuts the door behind us.

Chapter 4

Eddie and I are at the mall to pick up a present for Old Man Cheeto, who is going to be forty-eight years old this weekend and who is very healthy—probably from all those green beans and blue potatoes my mom has been cooking lately. Forty-eight is very old, if you ask me, and I am very happy with how Old Man Cheeto is holding up.

We are sitting in the food court and I have just explained to Eddie that yes, a half birthday isn't a whole birthday, but that it's still a very important day. We are finishing up a pretzel we had to split because it was the biggest pretzel in the world. Eddie leans over and wipes my mouth with a napkin because apparently I have cinnamon sugar around my lips. Once he gets my face all cleaned up, we are going to the bookstore because Eddie says that he knows just what our dad wants for his birthday this year, which is a book on history. "I thought that the whole point of growing up and finishing school is so you don't have to read books on history," I say.

"Dad says that after you grow up the *real* reading begins," Eddie tells me.

I want to know what that means, so I make a mental note to ask my dad when we get home, and then I think that I better wait until after his birthday or he'll know that Eddie and I were discussing books, and then he'll put two and two together and will figure out his present, which will take all the surprise right out of it.

Eddie holds my hand while we're walking through the mall and tells me to stay close so that we don't lose each other, which happened once a long time ago when I was very young and obviously Eddie's still not over it. I try to remind him that I was only on my own for five minutes, but Eddie says that's five minutes too long and holds my hand tighter. "Your mom still driving you and Victoria to school?" he says.

"Yep," I say, and then it's quiet between us.

Lately, on the way to school, my mom has been giving Victoria and me good-manners lessons. She says that it's important to ask people questions about themselves, about their lives. *"Don't just talk about yourself,"* she says.

I look at Eddie now and decide to practice being polite. "How's your mom and stepdad?" I ask him.

"Good, good," he says. "Everyone's fine."

We're passing my favorite cookie shop and I think about asking Eddie to stop and maybe get some cookies, but then I remember the size of that pretzel and decide to ask for cookies next time. "How's Bruno?" I say.

Eddie's face changes. "Bruno's getting old."

"I know."

He looks at me funny.

"What?" I say.

"Nothing," he says.

"What's wrong with Bruno?" I say.

On the way into the bookstore Eddie stops walking and crouches down so that his face is near my face. "Bruno is tired, and, well, Abigail Iris . . ."

"What?" I say.

"His days might be numbered."

"Numbered?" I say.

"He might be leaving us soon."

And my eyes tear up and I am trying hard not to cry and Eddie stands up and takes my hand and leads

me over to one of those cushy chairs they have in the corner and offers to buy me a hot chocolate.

"I don't want hot chocolate," I say. "I want Bruno to have many days left." And then I *am* crying and Eddie is telling me that *it's okay, it's okay, it's okay*, although we both know that if you have to say something three times, it's not true and it's anything *but* okay.

"I'm sorry, Abigail Iris," he says, patting my knee. "You don't even know Bruno that well. You only met our dog once. I thought I could tell you . . ." He puts an arm around my shoulder.

"I *should* know him," I say.

Victoria and I have been invited over to dinner by Eddie and Cameron's other parents but never got around to going. One night Victoria was having a sleepover and I didn't want to go without her, and another night was a family video movie night that we didn't want to postpone.

Now, though, with Bruno's days numbered,

I want to go to Eddie and Cameron's house for dinner, and I tell Eddie that. I also tell Eddie that I want to know what Bruno was like as a puppy. And he tells me that Bruno was so small when they first brought him home from the shelter that he fit in his dad's hand and that together he and Cameron, who were little boys then, could hold him, their two palms up, carefully supporting the tiny dog. He tells me that for the first few weeks, Bruno had to be bottle-fed because he was too little to eat for himself and that his mom sat on the couch, watching the news and feeding tiny Bruno with a baby bottle. He says that once Bruno was old enough to eat, he was old enough to shred blankets with his teeth and chase my brothers around the house, up and down the stairs, and into the backyard, where Bruno loved to play ball with the limes that had fallen from the tree. Hearing all these good stories about Bruno only makes me cry more, which makes Eddie seem very uncomfortable. "Please, Abigail Iris. Don't cry," he says.

"I can't help it," I say, sniffling.

"What if I tell you a secret?" he says. "I know what will make you feel better."

"Nothing can make me feel better," I say stubbornly.

"Dad told me that you're getting a kitten," he says in my ear.

"I am?" I say, feeling instantly better, if only a little bit. "Is it for sure? Is it a sure thing?"

"It's a sure thing, but it's a secret. Like the book we're buying Dad, you're not supposed to know. I only told you because you were crying. I wasn't supposed to let you know, Abigail Iris. Promise me you won't tell?"

"I promise, I promise," I say, and then I'm wiping my eyes and wanting to jump up from the cushy chair, happy and excited, and dance all around the store, but then I remember Bruno and his numbered days, and I don't go for the gusto. I look at Eddie and put my arm around him. Our arms are around each other and this is the way we stay, arm in arm through the store, up the stairs, and into the

History/Current Events section, where Old Man Cheeto's book is waiting.

While looking through the books, Eddie and I are approached by a very pretty girl with red hair and a name tag that says *Molly*, who asks us if we need help. "Our dad is a big reader," I say.

"That's great," she says.

"We're looking for a book on the Civil War," Eddie says.

"Our dad still reads even though he doesn't have to," I say.

She smiles at me. Then she smiles at Eddie, who seems suddenly shy. "My sister," he says, his face a little bit red, "she'll tell you anything."

"Really?" Molly says, looking right into Eddie's eyes.

"Hey," I say. "Can you help us find our dad's present?"

When Molly finds the book, she pulls it from the shelf and hands it to Eddie, who flips through it and admires the pages. And that's when the new book smell hits me and all those big words and all those smart ideas, and that's when I understand why Old Man Cheeto keeps reading even though he doesn't have to.

Eddie lets me hold Dad's book while we wait in line and asks me if I want to be the one to ask the woman behind the cash register about gift wrapping, which I do. The woman asks me if I want red paper or blue, paper with daisies or baseball bats or golf clubs or puppies or kittens, and of course, I want to say kittens, but it's Dad's book, Dad's day, Old Man Cheeto's forty-eighth, and so I say, "We'll take the baseball bat paper and a big blue bow!"

Chapter 5

Old Man Cheeto's birthday dinner is the same thing every year. My mother sets up a make-your-own-taco bar, with extra guacamole, in the middle of the dining room table. My dad is supposed to fill up his taco shells first because it's his birthday, but he has trouble being selfish and only fills up one shell even though we put four empty ones on his plate.

"Is there any plain chicken?" Victoria says, making a face at the chicken in taco sauce that my mother has piled high onto a little plate in the center of the table.

"Sorry, honey," my mother says. "I forgot."

"It's okay," Victoria says. "I'm thinking about

becoming a vegetarian anyway." She fills her shell only halfway with beans and cheese and a few pieces of lettuce.

"More for me," Cameron says, stuffing his shells so full of chicken, there's no room for anything else.

I fill one taco with beans and cheese, the other with chicken and guacamole. I put some lettuce and tomatoes on the side of my plate so my mother won't say anything about vitamins and health during Dad's birthday dinner.

"Well, happy birthday to me," my father says, raising his glass of lemonade. We all clink glasses with everyone, which requires a lot of adjusting chairs and reaching across the table.

"And happy almost half birthday to me," I say, but only Eddie reaches across the table to toast that one. "Does anyone have any announcements to make?" I ask.

"I got into Spring Select Soccer," Cameron says.

"That's great," my mother says.

"Really something," my father, the birthday boy, says.

"That's not the kind of announcement I had in mind," I say.

"Oh, did you have something to announce, honey?" my mother says.

I look at Eddie, who shakes his head *no* just the tiniest bit at me.

I look at the birthday boy, who is so happy with his birthday, he's smiling with his whole face, which shows off his wrinkles and makes him look younger at the same time. "I would just like to announce that you still barely look forty-seven in my opinion," I say. Then I take a bite from each of my tacos, trying to decide which one I prefer most today.

After dinner, my mother brings in the cake, and everyone makes a very big fuss over the way Victoria helped her decorate it with homemade icing flowers.

"I was at the mall buying your present, or I would have helped with the flowers," I say.

"We got you a very important book. It took Eddie and me a long time to pick it out."

"Abigail Iris," Eddie says. "Don't ruin it."

This is not my best moment, I must admit, ruining my dad's surprise and having Eddie get mad at me, both at the same time.

"No, no, it's still a surprise," Old Man Cheeto says, picking up the wrapped-up book from his pile of presents.

"A girl that worked there helped us find it. Her name was Molly, and she was very smiley at Eddie. I picked out the paper," I say. "They had kitten wrapping paper. But this seemed more boylike. Not that boys don't like cats. Many, many boys like cats," I can't help but add.

My father takes a long time opening his pile of gifts. Cameron gives him a smelly old baseball signed by someone very important that I've never heard of, and Victoria made him a special card with fancy writing on it. "It's calligraphy," she tells everyone. "Suitable for framing."

"It's lovely," my mother says, picking up the card and taking a special close-up look at it. "It's really beautiful."

"Open your book already," I say.

"Abigail Iris," my mother says. "Remember your manners."

"Please," I say. "Please open your book."

॰

"Still no Spot," I tell Rebecca at recess while we wait in line for our turn to jump rope. "Eddie said we were getting him, but maybe he was wrong."

"You can borrow Jazzy if you don't get your cat," she says.

"Thanks," I say, remembering my manners, but I don't want to borrow Jazzy. I want my own pet. I want Spot.

"You and your mother and Victoria are all invited to the baby's party," Rebecca says. "It's just for girls."

"That sounds like fun," I say, but Rebecca doesn't look like she agrees. It's her turn to jump rope, and she jumps away, straight up and down, without the little extra skip she usually does. Still, she's an excellent jumper and doesn't miss once. She just stops jumping when she's had enough and gets back in line to wait for her next turn.

Jumping rope is not my most preferred recess activity, but Genevieve and Cynthia have chosen to spend their recess weeding the Learning Garden by the kindergarten rooms, and I do not want my Only friend to feel completely deserted. My shoe catches on the rope on jump number four, and I grab Rebecca's arm and lead her over to the monkey bars, where we hang upside down like bats.

"Today is my half birthday," I tell my still-Only friend.

"Oh, happy half birthday, Abigail Iris," she says.

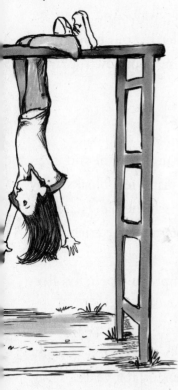

"Thank you," I say. "I hope it's a girl," Rebecca says, and for a minute I think she's talking about Spot, who is very much a boy I believe, and then I realize she's talking about the baby who's already having its own party and is not even born yet.

"Brothers are not completely awful," I say. I haven't seen Eddie for three days, not since our father's birthday dinner, since he's been at his other parents' house. I hope he isn't mad at me anymore for ruining the surprise of Old Man Cheeto's important book.

"Still," she says.

And, upside down or not, I nod in what I hope is an encouraging way. And then we spend the rest of recess letting our blood go to our heads and thinking our own private thoughts.

༄

My mother is late picking me up, and even though Billy Doil lives just a few blocks away and walks home by himself, he hangs around and waits with me after my Only friends are picked up.

"You have quite an impressive pencil collection," he says.

I have not thought of my pencils as a collection before, but maybe Billy Doil is right. "I've been collecting pencils for years," I say. "It's harder than it looks."

"I collect quarters," Billy Doil tells me. "Maybe sometime you could come over and see them. I have thirty-six out of the fifty states."

"Maybe," I say, thinking how weird it would be to go to Billy Doil's house after school. I remember what my dad said about Spot. "Maybe, not yes. There's a difference. Don't jump ahead."

"See you tomorrow, Abigail Iris," Billy Doil says when my mom drives up, and I wave good-bye and watch him turn to walk home.

I wonder if one of the students at the high school where my mom and my dad teach has been a troublemaker again and needed a talking to after school, and that's why my mom is late. She looks happy enough though, and she's in one of her singing-along-with-the-radio moods, so I don't bother to interrupt to find out.

We stop by the middle school, and Victoria is still talking to her friends when she gets in the car, and then starts text-messaging right away when the door shuts.

"And how was your day, honey?" I say.

"Stop it, Abigail Iris," she says. "Can't you see I'm doing something?"

"How green does green have to be?" I say to my mother when she stays stopped at a light after it changes.

"Oops," my mother says, and we jerk forward all at once.

We drop Victoria off at a friend's house so they can work on an important history report together, and she's still text-messaging when she gets out of the car and waves good-bye.

When we get home, I see Old Man Cheeto's car parked out front. It's a very pleasant surprise that he's home early and not busy being the yearbook adviser after school today, so I jump out of the car as soon as we park and run inside so I can give him a special Abigail Iris hello hug.

My dad's sitting on our special reading chair in the living room looking at the very important history book Eddie and I gave him for his birthday, which is very unusual for this time of day. I wonder why he's not in the kitchen starting dinner since he's home early or staring at a big pile of student work to grade at the kitchen table.

"Hey there, half-birthday girl," he says to me.

"You remembered," I say. I run over and am ready to do a flying leap when he holds his hand out in front of him and puts his book down on the arm of the chair.

"Shh," my father says. "I think someone's sleeping."

And that's when I see my best half-birthday present ever—Spot, curled up in a ball and asleep on Old Man Cheeto's lap.

Chapter 6

I am so excited to see Spot that I can barely keep myself from screaming and jumping up and down in the living room, but I do my best. I tiptoe over to my dad's chair with a smile so big I can feel it taking up my whole face. I'm not even sure I'm breathing. When I get up to the chair, I see Spot's wearing a big, weird collar around his neck and his little ears are sort of smashed against the plastic. "What have they done to my kitten?" I say, very worried and protective of little Spot.

"Shh," my dad says, whispering. "It's called an Elizabethan collar."

"I heard it was called a space collar," my mom says.

"When the vet handed Spot over, he called it Elizabethan," my dad says, shrugging.

"I don't care what it's called," I say. "What's it doing around my kitty's neck? Look at his ears."

My dad adjusts himself so that he gets a good look at Spot's ears, and then gently twists the collar, so that Spot's ears right themselves. "He had a little procedure," my dad says.

"Is he sick? Oh no! Bruno's days are numbered," I say, feeling myself about to cry.

My mom laughs. "He's just fine."

"Yep," Old Man Cheeto says. "A little groggy from the medicine. They said to expect him to perk up early this evening."

"Can I pet him?" I say.

"Of course," my mom says. "He's all yours."

"In fact, why don't you sit here with him," my dad says, carefully picking up a still-sleeping Spot and getting up from his chair.

I am so happy when I sit down and my dad

puts Spot in my lap. For a minute Spot opens his eyes to look at me, and then he goes right back to sleep. When I go to sniff the top of his head, my nose bumps into the collar, but still I can tell he smells clean and new and sweet. "He's safe here," I say. "I'll love him forever," I tell my parents.

❧

During our spaghetti-and-meatball dinner, I leave Spot on the chair but I check on him every few minutes to make sure that he's still sleeping and not feeling lonely. Victoria is staying for dinner at her friend's house, and my brothers aren't coming over for two more days, so it's just the three of us. My dad is telling us about his first cat, Elmer, and how he played fetch like a dog. "I was just your age," my dad says, looking at me. "Or wait, maybe I was ten. Yeah, I think I was ten."

"Tell us about fetch," my mom says, although I get the feeling she's heard this story before. "Tell Abigail Iris."

"I had this ring I'd made out of tinfoil and I'd toss it across the room and Elmer would run, pick it up with his mouth, and bring it back to me. He'd drop it at my feet or in my open palm. Most cats won't do that. It's a dog thing." My dad cuts a meatball in half with his fork and takes a bite.

"Maybe Spot will play fetch," I say.

"Maybe so," my mom says.

But my dad is somewhere else, chewing his meatball, still thinking about Elmer.

"You loved that cat," my mom says, reaching over and patting my dad's hand.

"Sometimes Elmer would want to play in the middle of the night, and in the morning, I'd wake up with that ring on my pillow. That was some cat," my dad says.

"Did Elmer have to wear a space collar when he was a kitten?"

"No," he says. "And that was a big mistake."

"I bet," my mom says, picking up her fork and twirling her noodles.

"Why?" I say.

"Well, there was a stray female cat who started spending time in our backyard, and soon we had little Elmers all over the place."

"That must have been fun," I say.

"Not really," he says, picking up his water glass and taking a sip. "It was hard to get them all adopted."

"What happened to them?" I ask.

"Your grandmother guilted your great-aunt into taking a couple of them, and we gave one to the neighbors. And we had to keep two."

"Did you get Elmer fixed after that?" my mom says.

"Fixed?" I say.

"Yep," my dad says. "Sure did." He laughs a little and reaches for a piece of garlic bread.

"Your sister is going to be so excited to see Spot," my mom says, smiling. Her smile is so pretty and she is so pretty too, I'm thinking, even with a circle of tomato sauce on her cheek.

"Honey," my dad says. "You've got something on your face." And he is wiping at his own face as a demonstration.

My mom picks up the napkin from her lap. "Where?" she says, wiping the wrong side.

"Let me get it," my dad says. "Here, let me." And he's leaning over the table toward her and she's leaning toward him. She's giving him her cheek and he's dabbing at the spot. "That's better," he says.

Because I received the best half-birthday present in the world, I'm not even sad that I don't have my own cake with my name written on it. I'm not even sad that we eat slices of my dad's leftover birthday cake instead. The cake is delicious, moist and sweet and creamy, but I eat it fast and don't even finish my whole piece or ask for anyone else's frosting because I want to get back to Spot. "Can I be excused?" I say. "Please, please."

My parents nod and I get up from the table. While I'm walking away, I hear a little sound coming from the living room, the tiniest meow ever. Spot is standing on all fours like he's been waiting for me and where have I been? And then he is sitting down and yawning and staring up into my face. "Hello," I say. I think about Bruno over at Eddie and Cameron's house and how his days are numbered and I feel sad for my brothers, but then I see Spot's adorable face, his green eyes, his furry little head cocked to one side in that silly collar, looking right at me, and I say, "This is just the beginning, Spot. Your days are not numbered. You and I have many, many, many days left together and we will make the most of them."

Chapter 7

The party for Rebecca's new brother or sister who is not born yet is at a very fancy outdoor restaurant. Even though the restaurant is just three blocks from my house, I have never eaten there. I'm sad for Rebecca that she's not going to be an Only much longer, but I'm a little excited about the shower since this is the first one I've ever gone to in my life. I kiss Spot good-bye on his nose.

"Get better, honey," my mother shouts up the stairs to Victoria, who has developed such a bad cold she has to miss the baby shower.

We are leaving Victoria alone at home, which is okay because she is in middle school and even babysits sometimes. My brothers will be over tomorrow, and I cannot wait to introduce them to Spot.

"Remember, Daddy's just over at Rebecca's house helping Henry set up the crib. Call him if you need anything," my mom says.

"I know, Mom," Victoria manages to shout from her bed. "You already told me."

"Okay, sweetie," my mom says, and then we walk out the door together in our dress-up sandals that make clacking noises on the sidewalk.

We have a whole section in the restaurant to ourselves, which is marked off by yellow ribbons and pink and blue balloons. The mothers have their own long table, and Rebecca's mom, Martha, is sitting at the very end of it with her chair pulled out to make room for her big belly.

I'm at the round children's table with Genevieve and Cynthia and Rebecca and Rebecca's cousin Joey, the only boy in the whole group of us. He's not the best example of a boy either. He's bouncing around so much, he knocks his chair over, and his mother has to leave the grown-up ladies table several times to make him sit back down. He's only three, but Rebecca glares at him like he should know better.

"Boy babies can be very sweet," I say, just in case Rebecca doesn't get her wish and ends up with a brother instead of a sister. For some reason, I get an image of what I think Billy Doil must have looked like as a baby, his hair shooting up straight in one spot the way it has since I've known him, which began in kindergarten. My mother calls it a cowlick when my brother Cameron has one first thing in the morning. She says cowlicks on boys are very endearing, but Cameron splashes water on his comb and flattens it down whenever she points it out.

"Grrrr," Joey says, showing all his teeth and making a monster face at me.

"*Some* boys can be very sweet," I say.

All the mothers are laughing at their table,

playing some kind of game that involves passing around folded up pieces of paper, and I think that for once it might be more fun to be at the grown-up table.

We are served our food one course at a time without even ordering first, which I think is almost as special as getting room service. The first course is cold raspberry soup. It's very red and the top of my soup is swirled around in a pattern, and there's some kind of leaf in the middle of it all. I can hear my mother going on and on about it at the adult table. "Oh, I just love raspberries," she says. "Isn't this special. This is so special. What a treat."

The raspberry soup is not a big hit at the children's table. Just my Only friend Genevieve eats hers, making a very big deal about dotting her mouth with her napkin after each spoonful. "Cold soup is very European," says Genevieve, who has actually been to France.

I have absolutely not been to France, but I smile at my mother when she looks over at me, so she thinks I'm enjoying my cold red soup when what I'm really wondering is why anyone would take a bunch of perfectly good raspberries and grind them up into mush.

I pick up the leaf from the middle of my bowl and sniff it and decide it smells a little bit like toothpaste.

"It's mint, Abigail Iris," my Only friend Cynthia says. "My mother grows it on our windowsill."

The windowsill makes me think of Spot, and I cannot believe I have not thought about him for nearly five whole minutes! The windowsill in our living room is his very favorite place in the world to sit in our house so far because he can look out into our front yard and search for possums and squirrels. The possums are bigger than he is, but Spot still growls low inside his body like he's sure he could catch one if we'd just open the front door and let him out into the world.

"After brunch, my mom says you can come over and meet Spot," I tell my three Only friends as the waiter takes away our raspberry soup. "He still has his space collar, but he's ready to receive visitors."

"Kids!" Rebecca's mother shouts from her place at the head of the long table. "Come join us. It's present time."

Joey knocks over his chair again and runs to his Aunt Martha like she's planning to give out actual presents instead of opening the baby's.

"Boys," Genevieve says.

"Babies," Rebecca says.

The presents are mostly clothes, which would be sort of boring even if they were for us, but the moms say things like "ooo" and "how cute" when Martha holds up each outfit.

My mother's face looks worried, and I bet she's thinking about our present, which may be the biggest box at the party but is not at all cute. I watched her wrap it this morning, so I know that inside that box is a special kind of diaper pail that doesn't let out even one bit of stink. "I always wanted one of these," my mother said as I passed her the tape.

"Oh, this is just perfect," Martha says when she finally unwraps our present, and I am glad to see my mother's face perk up a little.

"Such a clever design," Genevieve's mother says. "I just loved mine."

The waiter is busy bringing out our next

course, so we all go back to the kids' table, except for Joey, who is sitting on the ground crashing a tiny airplane into the diaper pail my mother gave Martha.

Where my soup bowl was before is now a fancy plate with a white-bread sandwich, no

crust, right in the middle of it. My mother and the other mothers are all talking about how beautiful their poached salmon looks.

"Just try your food, Abigail Iris," my mother practically shouts to me.

I take a big bite of my peanut butter and jelly.

I look over at Martha and she winks at me. Even if she is having another baby and changing my Only friend Rebecca's life, I decide right then that Martha is still a pretty good mom.

෴

My Only friends are so excited to meet Spot that they don't even ask me if my brothers are home, which is usually the first thing they do when they come to my house.

Each of us has something special at her house. Genevieve has a hot tub that's almost big enough to swim in. Cynthia has a swinging chair that hangs from the ceiling of her bedroom. Rebecca has a trampoline in her backyard. And I have my half brothers, Eddie and Cameron, who are with us half of the time, and now I have a new kitten, too.

"I brought you a piece of cake," I say to Victoria, who is lying on the living room couch now. "Sorry you had to miss the party."

Victoria's eyes are squinty shut and she has piled up so many tissues on the coffee table, it looks like she's made a little sculpture out of them. My father says that Victoria is very dramatic sometimes, and he hopes I don't get that way when it's my turn to be an almost-teenager and go to middle school.

"Thanks, Abigail Iris," she says to me, sitting up a little and taking a bite, and I feel bad for thinking about her being dramatic sometimes because she really does look pretty sick with her cold.

"Where's Mom?" she says.

"She's coming," I tell her. "We ran ahead."

Victoria hands me the rest of the cake and lies back down.

"Oh, he's very, very, very cute," Cynthia says.

"Just adorable," Genevieve says.

"Way better than a new baby," Rebecca says.

Obviously, my Only friends have found Spot. He has actually turned away from the window to look at them. "Would you like to hold him?" I ask.

"Yes!" they all start shouting and I have to tell them to calm down because they will get Spot way too excited. Then I give them each a turn, my three Only best friends. And I make sure they are gentle as they hold my kitten, one at a time.

Chapter 8

The good thing about Victoria's cold, my mom says, is that it doesn't seem to be contagious. Usually when one of us gets sick, we all get sick, maybe not all at the same time but one by one. Even Eddie and Cameron, who only live here half the time, have been known to come down with whatever cold or flu is going around in this house.

My mom has decided that right after the six o'clock news ends, my dad and I should go to the drugstore to buy Victoria some medicine for her very stubborn cold. The cold is what my dad calls a hanger-on. My sister has been sick for over a week and hasn't been to school in three days. She's on the couch, lying down, and taking up nearly the whole thing, which is a privilege you get in this family only when you're sick, at least if you're a kid. Sometimes, if Old Man Cheeto has had what my mom calls a particularly harrowing day, he gets the privilege even when he's not sick. The taking-up-the-whole-couch privilege is one that I greatly appreciate and believe in when *I'm* the sick one, but now that I'm sitting on the floor, I think we need a new policy around here.

My mom and dad are sitting in the big blue chairs and Spot, his space collar finally gone, is the cutest, sweetest kitten in the world. He's sleeping at the foot of the couch, with one paw across his face and over his eyes.

These are the things I've learned about Spot.

1. He is a very good sleeper.
2. He has favorite places in the house to do all that sleeping.

3. One of his favorite places is the foot of the couch, where he is now.
4. Another favorite spot is Old Man Cheeto's chest.
5. He also likes the gray cushion on Victoria's desk chair.
6. He prefers chicken to fish.
7. He is very open to trying people food, but my mom has a policy about not sharing our dinner with him.
8. He loves me best, but Victoria is apparently his second favorite person in this family, and my dad comes in a close third.

"I think Spot is the cutest cat I've ever seen," Victoria says now, and then she sits up and pets his head. And then she moans and falls back very dramatically and closes her eyes. "I feel terrible," she says. "This is the worst cold," she announces.

"Poor girl," my dad says.

"What can I get you, Vickie?" my mom says, leaning toward her.

"I can't eat anything," my sister says.

"Does your stomach hurt?" my mom wants to know.

My sister shakes her head. And then she sneezes.

"Bless you," I say from the floor.

"Thanks," she says.

During a commercial, my mom says something in a whispery voice to my dad and my dad just shakes his head and says, "We don't know that yet."

"What don't we know?" I say.

"Nothing, honey," my mom says, and she gives my dad one of those looks.

"What don't we know?" my sister says, and then she sneezes, not once, but three times in a row.

୫

Even though I can do it myself, my dad likes to fasten my seat belt, so he's leaning over me and searching for the second half of the belt, which seems to be hiding. "Where is it?" he says, more to himself than to me. "There you are," he says, finding it.

"I can do it," I say.

"I like to hear the click, Abigail Iris," he says, and then we both listen for it.

When we pull into the parking lot, I remind him that Victoria and I both prefer the grape cough syrup over the cherry syrup. And my dad reminds me that my sister doesn't have a cough.

"Oh," I say.

"She's mostly congested," he says.

"And her eyes are red," I add.

"This is a very picky bug," my dad says. "It's a bug that likes your sister, but doesn't like you." He winks at me. "I like you though."

"You don't like me," I correct him. "You *love* me."

"Good point," he says.

My dad and I walk into the drugstore holding hands. When we pass the ice-cream

counter, I squeeze his hand, and before I can even get the words out, he promises me a scoop when we're done. And yes, I'm concerned about my sick sister, but I'm also trying to make a decision between my two favorite flavors. Part of me wants mint chip but part of me wants cookies and cream, which I think is almost like getting two desserts in one cup.

At the back of the store, my dad talks to a woman in a blue smock and I listen while he describes Victoria's symptoms. Headache, stuffed-up nose, and red eyes. The woman is very old, I think, and her lipstick is bright orange. She wears glasses that hang from a chain around her neck. While my dad talks, she lifts the glasses from her chest and puts them on, like they might help her with hearing him. My dad tells her that Victoria has been feeling like this for nearly two weeks, and the pharmacist's eyes get big.

"No cough?" she says.

My dad shakes his head.

"No chills, body aches?"

My dad shakes his head again.

"Any new animals introduced to the home?" she says.

"Well . . . ," my dad says.

"Well?" she says.

My dad looks at me and then the woman looks at me.

"What?" I say, dropping my dad's hand.

"Any new animals?" the woman repeats.

"Actually, yes," he admits.

And then it clicks, as loud and certain as the seat belt, and I don't even need to hear the word "allergies" leave the woman's lips, before my eyes start to spill over with tears.

"Sweetheart," my dad says, bending down.

"Spot is a member of our family," I say.

"Don't cry, sweetheart," my dad says. "Let's get you two scoops of ice cream."

"No," I say.

"I'm sorry, Abigail Iris," he says. "Let's get some ice cream."

"I'm not hungry," I tell him. And suddenly it's true. If you put a bowl of cookies and cream *and* mint chip in front of me, I wouldn't be able to eat a bite.

⁂

"We don't know anything for sure, Abigail Iris," my dad says on the way home. Even though I told him I didn't want any ice cream, he bought a whole half gallon of each of my favorite flavors. The white bags sit beside me in the backseat and I am not at all interested in them. I'm trying not to cry because I know that my dad feels badly about what the woman said about Victoria and Spot, but it's nearly impossible. "Maybe Victoria can go live somewhere else," I say, and my dad's eyes catch mine in the rearview mirror.

"You don't mean that," he says.

"Maybe she can just stay in our bedroom when she's home."

"Abigail Iris," he says.

"They don't have to see each other," I insist.

"You know that's impossible."

"How about a gas mask?"

"A what?" he says.

"I saw someone on the news wearing a gas mask. It looked like a very smart thing to do," I say.

I can't see my dad's mouth, but I can see his eyes in the rearview mirror, and they look like they're almost smiling.

"Spot is a family member too," I say again.

"Abigail Iris, sweetheart," he says. "We'll figure something out."

Chapter 9

There's a huge wooden stork carrying a blue blanket in its beak stuck right in the middle of my Only friend Rebecca's front lawn. My mother parks the car by the curb right in front of it.

"'Stephen Jeremy, eight pounds, nine ounces, twenty inches,'" my mother says aloud, reading the fancy writing on the stork's blanket. I already know how big the baby is because Rebecca's dad told my mom on the phone yesterday, and my mother announced the details to anyone who would listen.

"I can read cursive," I tell my mother.

"I know you can, Abigail Iris. I'm just so

excited," she says to me. "I can't think of anything more exciting than a new baby, can you?"

I can think of many things more exciting—inventing a cure for Victoria's allergies, for one thing. But I just shrug.

I am in a grumpy, grumpy mood. Spot is locked away in my parents' bedroom until we can figure out what to do next, and I am supposed to smile at my Only friend's new baby when what I would prefer to do is spend every single second with Spot, who does not make me even in the least bit sick.

"Do you want to carry the balloons?" my mother asks.

"Okay," I say, and I take the big bunch from her and get out of the car. I am in such a bad mood I think I could let the balloons go, but I decide they're too special and hold on tight. The balloons are blue and there is a big teddy bear balloon in the center.

My mother is carrying a cinnamon noodle casserole, my grandmother's special noodle kugel recipe, that my mother made this morning while Old Man Cheeto and I played with Spot in their bedroom. The whole house smelled good while she cooked, but I pretended not to notice.

"I doubled the recipe. There's one waiting for us at home for dinner," my mother says to me now, reading my mind the way she has a disturbing habit of doing.

"I'm not hungry," I say, which isn't exactly true. The casserole must still be a little warm because the cinnamon smell of it is leaking through the plastic wrap.

"I'm sorry about Spot," my mother said. "Your father and I had no idea Victoria was so allergic to cats. She must have inherited the allergy from Grandma."

"Maybe Victoria could go live with her," I suggest.

"Abigail Iris," my mother says, frowning at me.

"It was just a suggestion," I say.

"You understand that it's not her fault,

honey. I think Victoria's almost as upset about the whole thing as you are."

"I don't know. I'm pretty upset," I say.

"Remember, she was almost as excited about Spot as you were."

"I don't know. I was pretty excited," I say.

My mom laughs a little.

"It's not funny, Mom."

My mom stops laughing and gives me a serious look. "I know, honey. You both were excited. We all were."

"I guess," I say.

When Rebecca's father, Henry, opens the door, my mother is smiling again, and I am, too. I even mean it a little. It is hard not to be excited that Rebecca's baby brother has finally arrived. Rebecca's father is wearing pajama bottoms and a T-shirt, and his face looks like my dad's does when he takes a vacation from shaving.

"The little prince is napping, I believe," Rebecca's father whispers. "Come right on in."

Martha is half sitting up, half lying on the

couch with the tiny new baby snuggled up against her chest. She waves and gives us a big smile hello. The baby is wearing a tiny white undershirt and a diaper. The side of his face that I can see is red, and his eyes are closed. His hair is a black splotch on top of his head. He isn't all that much bigger than Spot, and seeing him makes me miss my kitty snuggled up against me right now.

"Oh, he's so sweet," my mother says. "Look at those little toes. He's just perfect."

"Are those for Stephen?" Martha says, nodding at my balloons.

"Who?" I say.

"The baby," my mother reminds me.

"Oh, right," I say. Of course, no one actually expects me to hand the baby the balloons, but I'm not sure what to do with them because Martha's hands are wrapped around him. I finally give the balloons to my mother. "I'm going upstairs to see Rebecca, okay?" I say.

"She'd love that, honey," Martha says.

I knock gently on my Only friend's bedroom door. Her parents turned their office into the baby's room, so she's lucky and gets to keep her own room.

"Who is it?" Rebecca says.

"Just me," I say, opening the door.

"Did you see him?" she says.

I nod.

Rebecca is lying on her bed reading, and I can see right away that it's not even a schoolbook. Rebecca is an excellent reader. "He's a boy," she says, putting her book down. "And he's all red and wrinkly."

"I thought he was sort of cute," I say.

"I guess," she says.

I lie down on the bed next to my no-longer-Only friend Rebecca. "Remember Victoria's awful cold?" I say. "Well, it turns out she doesn't have a cold at all. She's allergic to Spot, and we have to do something." I feel my eyes fill up.

"Oh, Abigail Iris," Rebecca says to me. "That's terrible. What are you going to do?"

"I don't know," I say. "My mother says Victoria can't take allergy medicine every day, that it's not good for a growing girl."

"That's too bad," Rebecca says. "Come on. Let's go bounce."

Outside, we stop to pet Rebecca's dog, Jazzy, who is taking his little afternoon nap in the shade, and then we climb up on her trampoline and jump up and down holding hands until we're both smiling again.

When we walk back in through the kitchen, we pass Rebecca's dad, who's sitting at the table, digging a fork into the cinnamon noodle kugel, eating right from the pan.

"Daddy!" Rebecca says.

"Oh, you caught me. Delicious, Abigail Iris," he says.

"I'm glad you like it," I say, suddenly a little sad I didn't help my mother cook the way I sometimes do.

In the living room, the baby is still sleeping on Martha's chest, but now he's covered in a blanket. My mother is sitting on the couch next to them, and I think she looks kind of lonely without anyone little sleeping on her, so, even though I am eight and a half years old, I decide to sit on her lap. Martha pats the space next to her, and Rebecca sits down there.

"Rebecca, you're a sister now, just like Abigail Iris," my mother says. "You girls will have even more to talk about."

The baby starts squirming around on Martha's chest and making catlike noises. "Someone's hungry," Martha says.

"That's probably our cue," my mother says, lifting me off of her lap and standing up.

"Next time you come visit, he'll be a little

older and you can hold Stephen if you want to, Abigail Iris," Martha says.

"Thank you," I say, even though I think I'd prefer to jump on the trampoline with Rebecca.

"Just call if you need anything. Anything at all," my mother says. "I'm going to bring the rest of the clan over next time if that's okay. 'Bye, Henry!" she shouts toward the kitchen.

Rebecca is being very helpful, getting her mother a glass of water and finding a new pack of diapers, so I shout good-bye to her, too, and then follow my mother to the car.

We're almost home when my mother's cell phone rings, and I dig around in her purse until I find it and answer it.

"He's finally gone," my father says.

"Who?" I say. "Who's gone?"

"What is it, Abigail Iris?" my mother says. "What's happening?"

"Abigail Iris?" my father says into the phone. "Did you answer your mother's phone again?"

"Yes," I say. "But I'm supposed to. She's driving."

"Eddie and Cameron's old dog," my father says. "He's finally gone."

"Gone where?" I say, but then I remember about Eddie saying Bruno's days were numbered, and I understand. "Oh," I say, feeling sad. I explain to my mom, who nods but doesn't say anything.

When I get inside the house, I run right to my parents' bedroom and find my little brand-new kitten asleep in the exact center of the big bed. I have so many feelings all at once that when I curl up with Spot, I think I might actually go to sleep even though it's only four thirty in the afternoon.

Eddie and Cameron were supposed to come over tonight, but because of Bruno being gone, they decided to stay at their other house and come over tomorrow instead. It's just the four of us at the dinner table with a whole big noodle kugel in front of us. My mother is going on and on about Stephen and how sweet and perfect his toes and fingers are and how happy Martha seems. I can't help but notice that Victoria's eyes are prettier now that they're not red and puffy. I think about what my mother said about Victoria's allergies not being her fault and how she was almost as excited about Spot's arrival as I was. I clear my throat several times until my mother finally stops talking, and everyone, even Victoria, looks at me.

"Yes?" my father says.

"I know you would much prefer not to be allergic to Spot," I say.

"Okay," my sister says cautiously. "And?"

"I know you can't help taking after Grandma," I say. "That's all."

Then I take the last bite of my noodle kugel and ask for seconds.

Chapter 10

Eddie has a new friend and he's bringing her over this afternoon so I can meet her—well, not really meet her, because I've met her before. She's Molly from the bookstore, and she helped us pick out Old Man Cheeto's birthday present. Eddie and Cameron and Molly are coming over for lunch, and we're all going to sit and eat outside, which is my favorite place to eat on a sunny day. My mom and dad have been having serious discussions about what to do about Spot because apparently he can't stay in their bedroom forever, although I think it's working out just fine.

My dad says it's been a rough couple of days but wants me to look on the bright side of things. He tells me that Bruno is buried in my brothers' backyard right under the lime tree where he played when he was a puppy. Bruno had a big, long life and lots of toys and a whole family who paid attention to him. He got the best dog food and sometimes the family let him eat scraps from the dinner table. He says that Bruno's now in a spot where he will smell those limes always.

He also reminds me that Spot is very sociable and not afraid of people and has many more days in front of him, which really means that he'll get along great with some other family for a very long time.

My parents looked sad when they were talking about Bruno, and serious and stressed when they were talking about Spot, so I tried not to argue too much and gave them what my sister calls *mental space*.

Once Eddie called and asked my mom if he could bring a new friend to lunch, though, my mom's face relaxed. "A visitor will do us all good," she said, hanging up the phone. "Let's make a big salad and turkey sandwiches."

"Good idea," my dad said, slapping his thighs and getting up from the couch.

"I'll help," I said.

༃

When we hear the car pull up to the curb, my dad puts down the avocado he's getting ready to slice and my mom puts down the lemon she's been squeezing into the pitcher of iced tea, and the three of us head toward the front door.

"I sort of already know Molly," I say proudly.

"You do?" my dad says.

"That's right," my mom says. "You were there the day they met."

Victoria, who is no longer sick now that Spot is locked up like a prisoner in my parents' bedroom, rushes down the stairs to meet Molly too. Apparently this Molly person is very important, I'm thinking, and so I put on my best smile when I say hello.

Molly looks different than she did at the bookstore, even prettier than I remember. Her reddish brown hair is shiny, and she's wearing it down instead of up in a ponytail. "Hi, everyone," she says.

"We're happy to meet you," my mom says, putting out her hand for Molly to shake.

"Welcome, welcome," my dad says. "I'm enjoying the book."

Molly smiles and shakes my mom's hand, and then shakes my dad's hand, and then shakes Victoria's hand, and then leans down finally to shake mine.

"Nice to see you again, Abigail Iris," she says.

"Your hair is very pretty," I say.

"How sweet," she says.

"How about some sun tea, Molly?" my mom asks.

"That would be great," she says, so I rush into the kitchen to pour her a glass.

⅗

While my parents are preparing the sand-wiches, I grab Molly's hand, lead her out of the living room, and tell her there's one last family member for her to meet. Eddie, who seems to like his new friend very much and hasn't left her side, follows us.

"I want to hang out with Spot too," Cameron says.

"Everyone's welcome," I say.

"Where are we going?" Molly asks.

"Spot's hidden away," I tell her.

"He's what?" she says.

"He makes my sister sick," I say.

"Allergies," Victoria says. She's standing on the stairs and looks like she hasn't decided whether she's going up or coming down. "I wish I could hang out with Spot."

"I wish you could too," I say, and mean it.

"She gets it from her grandmother," my mom shouts from the kitchen.

"Give Spot a hug from me, and let me know when lunch is ready," my sister says, turning and walking slowly up the stairs.

Once the door to my parents' bedroom is closed and I know Victoria is out of earshot, I complain a little about her sneezing, even though I feel sorry for her. My brothers let me talk, looking at me now and then, nodding sympathetically. Eddie sits on the bench at the foot of the bed and Molly stands next to him. Cameron and I sit on the bed and watch Spot, who is just now waking up from yet another nap. "He's a very good sleeper," I tell them.

When Molly leans down to pet Spot's head, her pretty red hair falls in front of her face. Spot reaches up to bat at her hair like it's the best toy he's ever seen.

"He's so cute," Molly says. "Look at that spot on his nose."

"It looks like paint," Cameron says.

"About Victoria's allergies . . . ," I say.

"What about them?" Eddie says.

I lean in. "Well . . . ," I say, whispering.

"What?" Cameron says.

"At first, I thought there were some dramatics involved," I say, which is a phrase my

mom uses when I don't like her cooked carrots or green beans and I let my face show it.

"Sneezing and red eyes aren't her fault, Abigail Iris," Eddie says.

"I know that now," I say, and scratch under Spot's chin.

"I'm allergic to chocolate," Molly says.

And then I think about a life without chocolate and feel very sorry for her. "How can you live like that?" I want to know.

"I eat vanilla," she says, smiling.

"You're allergic to certain flowers, Cameron," Eddie says.

"Lucky I'm a guy," Cameron says.

"Don't lie," Eddie says, play-hitting him on the shoulder. "You know you like flowers."

"I sort of do," Cameron admits.

And then we all laugh.

Spot is chasing a little gray mouse that has Velcro on its belly. Earlier my dad opened up the mouse's belly and put some catnip inside and even though Spot isn't supposed to be fully in love with catnip until he's a little bigger, he seems to like it very much. He hits the mouse with his paw and sends it flying and then he chases it around the bedroom.

"I want to play," Cameron says suddenly, standing up. He goes over to the corner and snatches the mouse, then tosses it to the opposite end of the room. Spot leaps in the air, dashing across the bedroom, and snatches up the mouse in his mouth. He looks at Cameron and cocks his little head. "Bring it back," Cameron says.

And then Spot trots over to my brother and lets the mouse drop at Cameron's feet.

"He's like Dad's old cat," Eddie says, excited. "He plays fetch!"

"Does Dad know?" Cameron asks, looking at me.

I shake my head. "I don't think he's ever done that before. Do it again," I say. And Cameron picks up the mouse and tosses it one more time. It bounces off the closet door and lands on the rug. Immediately, Spot rushes over, snatches it up in his mouth, trots back, and drops it at Cameron's feet again.

"Unbelievable," Eddie says. "I always thought Dad was exaggerating."

"Yeah, everyone says their cat is a dog-cat, not a cat-cat, but Spot might truly be a little bit of both," Molly says.

"I want to take this cat home," Eddie says.

And I look at him.

And Cameron looks at him.

And Molly looks at him.

"You want to take Spot home?" I ask, and

then I'm full of many feelings at once. But there's a knock on the door before I can even think through and name those feelings.

"Lunch is ready," my mom says. "Come and get it."

Chapter 11

I watch how Molly eats her sandwich and decide I will eat exactly the same way when I'm visiting a new friend's family. First she says how beautiful everything looks. Then she says how wonderful everything tastes. And then she remembers to chew slowly, with her mouth closed.

I look at Victoria to see if even she's impressed, but she just squints at me with her very clear, not itchy eyes and says, "What are you staring at?"

"Nothing," I say. "What a delicious looking and tasting sandwich," I tell Old Man Cheeto and my mother.

"Why, thank you, Abigail Iris," my father says.

"Yes, thank you, honey," my mother says.

"Chew with your mouth closed," Victoria says.

I'd prefer to stick out my tongue at Victoria, but I remember our special company is present at the table, and that means manners or no dessert. So, instead, I close my mouth and try to chew like I know something very important that no one else is allowed to know. This is the one good trick my Only friend Cynthia learned at the Mini Manners class her mother forced her to take over Spring Break.

I am smiling at our company, but in my head I am working out what my Only friend Genevieve would call Plan B, and what I have secretly named The Pet Project. Plan B is obviously not nearly as good as Plan A but not nearly as bad as The Answer Is No. According to Genevieve, if you absolutely cannot make your case, you must come up with Plan B on your own, or you will be forced into The Answer Is No, which in this case would mean No Spot, something I refuse to consider.

While I am plotting The Pet Project, Cameron and Eddie are going on and on about Spot and how he can play fetch just like the cat our dad had when he was a kid.

"That's unbelievable," my dad says.

"What are the chances of that," my mother says, but her face looks more sad than delighted. Probably she's thinking what I would be thinking if it weren't for Plan B, that this is one more wonderful thing we have to know about Spot before he leaves us forever.

I tap my fork against my glass of sun tea, hoping it will make a lovely tinkling sound and everyone will look at me. Instead, I start to knock the glass over and quickly pick it back up and blot the little bit of spilled tea with my napkin.

"What's going on over there?" Cameron says.

"I have an announcement to make," I say.

"An announcement?" my mother says, raising her eyebrows at me. "In front of our company?"

"Our company already knows about it," I say.

"I do?" Molly says, pushing her shiny hair behind her ears, which I now see are sparkly with gold earrings.

"Yes," I say. "It was almost Molly's idea."

"It was?" Eddie says.

"Sort of," I say.

"Then I'm sure it's a good one. Let's hear it, Abigail Iris," my father says.

"Spot is considering going to live with Eddie and Cameron at their other house," I say.

"Really? He is?" Cameron says.

"Yes, he is," I say.

"I don't know," my father says.

"It's the best Plan B ever!" I say. "Why don't you know?"

"I think some other adults need to be consulted first, honey," my mother says.

"Who?" I say.

"Eddie and Cameron's other parents," Victoria says. "Obviously."

"Oh," I say, thinking that the "obviously" was not necessary in front of our company. Of course, I see Cameron and Eddie's parents once in a while when they drop off Cameron and Eddie or pick them up, but these are not adults I think about very often.

"It may be a little soon," my mother says.

"Soon?" I say. "I thought we had to do

something right away because of the terrible allergies Victoria inherited from Grandma."

"Soon after Bruno, honey," Old Man Cheeto says softly.

"Oh," I say again. And then we are all very quiet for a minute, thinking about Bruno and his numbered days, which have now ended.

"It would be too soon for a new dog, but maybe not a new cat," Eddie says.

"Even a dog-cat," Cameron says.

Then everyone is talking all at once about Spot again and what a very special kitten he is, and my mother's face is relaxing a little, and she looks like she might want to smile again one day soon.

❧

At school the next day, Henry decides to bring his daughter and her three best friends—which includes me—lunch to celebrate the new baby. Also, there was nothing in their refrigerator to pack but casseroles.

This is what he told my mom when Henry

called our house at seven thirty that morning. My mother is very organized and had made my sandwich the night before, the way she always does, but I heard her say on the phone, "Yes. No, not yet. How fun." Then she put my brown bag right back in the refrigerator for the next day and told me Henry was bringing a special treat today.

Henry is on leave from work for the first three weeks of the new baby's life, but even though he isn't working, he doesn't look very rested in my opinion. He's waiting for us at the outdoor picnic tables at lunch period, and for a minute I think he's asleep at the table sitting up, but when we run up to him, he perks right up and starts opening containers of Chinese food and telling us to help ourselves.

"Is that chicken?" I ask, pointing at a carton full of food that looks vaguely familiar.

"I think it's beef," Cynthia says.

"Let's see," Henry says, peering in the carton. "That looks like the tofu to me," he says as if he's just as confused as we are.

"Bean curd," Genevieve says, "is a perfect protein." She dips her chopsticks in the carton and puts two very large pieces of it on her plate.

Billy Doil has managed to sit down right next to me. He unwraps his sandwich and takes a bite. "You guys having takeout?" he says.

"Looks that way," Genevieve says, and I'm thinking she doesn't have to be quite so mean to Billy even if it isn't the best question.

I help myself to some white rice and work at picking up individual pieces of it with my chopsticks, which is not nearly as easy as it looks. Then I decide to go for the gusto, and I help myself to a heaping spoonful of everything and use a fork to take a big bite of each of Henry's selections.

Rebecca is practically sitting on her dad's lap across from me, and I am wishing my dad could skip teaching school one day and bring me an almost surprise lunch, too.

But even though my dad can't bring me lunch, I remind myself that he does take me out for ice cream after school sometimes

before we settle down and do our homework together at the kitchen table.

"How's Stephen Jeremy?" I ask, proud that I remembered his entire name in the right order.

"He's not much of a sleeper. I can tell you that much, Abigail Iris," Henry says.

"Was I a good sleeper, Dad?" Rebecca asks. "Was I a better sleeper?"

"Geez, honey. I don't really remember," Henry says. "It's hard to remember any of this newborn baby stuff."

Rebecca inches a little away from her dad, shoves a spoonful of something red and gooey into her mouth, and then pouts.

Wrong answer, I'm thinking.

"I was a terrible napper," Billy Doil says.

"Really?" Henry says.

"Yep," Billy Doil says, munching away on his carrot sticks now. "I stopped napping completely when I was eighteen months old."

"Is that right?" Henry says, looking nervous.

When it's fortune cookie time, my two still-Only friends read their fortunes aloud.

"'You will see your name in lights,'" Cynthia reads.

"'You have a deep appreciation of art and music,'" Genevieve reads.

Rebecca finally cheers up a little when she reads hers. "'Something you lost will soon be found.' That has to be Dilly," Rebecca says. Dilly is one of her favorite stuffed animals, and he's often temporarily missing, so this is a pretty good guess. He's usually hiding under her covers somewhere.

"What's yours say, Abigail Iris?" Billy Doil asks.

I'm focusing so hard on my fortune, trying

to figure out what it means, that he has to elbow me and ask again before I answer.

"'May life throw you a pleasant curve,'" I read. "What does that mean, Henry?"

"It means plan to be surprised, I guess," he says. Then he yawns very loudly and doesn't even bother covering his mouth. "Sounds like an excellent plan to me."

Chapter 12

When you adopt a kitten, you make a commitment, and even if your sister is allergic to Spot and sneezing and carrying on, you have to think about that commitment before you find him a new home. When you adopt a kitten from the Second Chance Rescue group, you sign a piece of paper that says you'll inform the group about any change of plans and won't just give Spot away.

"How would they ever know?" I ask my mom.

"That's not the point," she says. "They trusted us."

"Oh."

"I signed on the dotted line."

"You're a good person," I say.

She smiles at me, laughs a little, and says, "And you're a good girl, Abigail Iris."

I think about almost letting all of Stephen Jeremy's balloons fly away. I think about how I used to blame Victoria for the allergies Grandma gave her. "Sometimes," I say.

"*Most* of the time," my mom says.

It's Saturday morning and my mom is on the phone with the cat-rescue woman. She's telling her about Victoria's allergies and about Bruno. She tells the woman that because Bruno's no longer with us, there's a vacancy at Eddie and Cameron's other house. She explains that Spot will still be a part of our family and that I, in fact, will be visiting him regularly.

The cat-rescue woman would like my mom to come to the farmers' market tomorrow morning to talk about this in person, which I think is a very good idea because then we can get some of that fresh, hot sourdough bread and maybe some more of those blue potatoes.

I am surprised that the Fuji apple man isn't at his stand, and instead there's his son holding a tray of sliced Red Delicious apples. He looks like he's Cameron's age, and he says, "Sweet as sugar," in a voice very much like his dad's.

"Something new," my mom says. My mom sees me eyeing the tray and she nudges me forward, saying, "Go ahead, Abigail Iris, take one."

And I do.

While I'm chewing and deciding whether or not this Red Delicious apple is delicious enough to ask my mom to bring a few of them home, my mom asks the boy questions.

"How's your dad?" my mom wants to know.

And he tells us that his dad is now a grandfather and that he's at the hospital with his new granddaughter, Lucy. He tells us that Lucy was born with a full head of hair and that she weighs nearly nine pounds.

"You're an uncle," my mom says, excited.

"That's right," he says. "I'm Uncle Joey."

"How wonderful," my mom says. "Send your family our best wishes."

After we leave the apple stand, I steer my mom over to the popcorn stand for a quick sample and tell her that I think Lucy is a very cute name for a baby girl.

"It is!" she agrees. She's carrying four Red Delicious apples in a brown bag and she's talking to me about what a nice man the Apple Man is and how terrific it is that he's a grandfather. "He's wanted a grandchild for years," my mom says.

I am always amazed at how much my mom knows about people and make a mental note to become a better listener so that I can know a lot too.

Before we reach the Second Chance Rescue booth, my mom reminds me that I can look at the kittens, but that I probably shouldn't pet them or pick them up. "We can't take any home and it will just make you sad," she says.

"I know," I say.

"Just remember," she says.

Still, I stare at the kittens and listen to their little meows while my mom tells the rescue woman all about Cameron and Eddie and their parents. She says she doubts very much that Spot will be declawed and that he'll never, ever spend the night outside in the rain.

She tells her again about Bruno and what a great life he had in that house.

"Bruno was beloved," I chime in, which is something I heard my dad say to my mom the day he died.

"Okay," the woman says, smiling at me. "Sounds good," she says.

"We love Spot," my mom says.

"These things happen," the woman says, sweetly. She hands my mom the clipboard. "Just fill out the bottom half."

"Of course," my mom says.

॰

My dad and I are going to Eddie and Cameron's other house with Spot for a visit. I am going to be looking at their house and other parents very carefully because it is important that Spot goes to a good home. Still, it is a sad day for me, even though he's just visiting, because we all know what comes next: the big move. My dad has already placed a new litter box and food bowl and a big bag of cat food and a few of Spot's toys in the backseat, but he's kept the mouse with the Velcro belly to toss into the cat carrier and a couple of cat treats to minimize Spot's discomfort on the road.

"For the most part, cats hate cars," my dad tells me.

"Even a dog-cat?" I say.

"Even a dog-cat," he says

When we get to Eddie and Cameron's house, we're greeted by Eddie and his mom, who's waving and smiling from the doorway. She's wearing jeans and a T-shirt and an apron and tennis shoes. I've met her a few times, but only briefly, and I've never been inside my brothers' other house. My dad calls her Kathy, and it's strange to think that they were married before.

"Hello, Abigail Iris," she says warmly.

"Hello," I say.

"You're all grown up," she tells me, which isn't exactly true because I expect to get much taller in the future. I want to say, "I've got a lot of growing to do, Kathy," but I don't tell her this. Instead I just smile.

After Eddie hugs us hello, he takes the cat carrier from my dad and leads us into the house. "Come on in," he says.

"Yes, yes," Kathy says.

We follow Eddie and Kathy inside and I am very happy that the house is pretty and comfortable-looking at the same time. There are big, fat couches in the living room and a newspaper spread out on the coffee table, which is one of Spot's favorite things to stand on. They lead us into the kitchen, which smells like cinnamon, and I can see the lime tree out the sliding glass door.

"I made you some cookies," Kathy says, looking at me.

Eddie sets the cat carrier on the table and Spot meows and rubs his face against the bars.

"He wants to meet everyone," I say.

Just then Eddie's other dad comes down the stairs, smiling big and saying hello.

"How are you, Max?" my dad asks.

"Can't complain," Max says, and the two of them shake hands.

After the handshake, Max looks at the cat carrier. "This must be the infamous Spot," he says, bending down and getting a look inside.

Eddie leans forward and slides the little door open.

Spot doesn't seem scared at all, doesn't seem to think twice before stepping out of the carrier and greeting everyone with another meow.

"He's adorable," Kathy says.

"And so friendly," Max says.

"Spot is a very special cat. He's a dog-cat, but he still doesn't like cars," I say.

"Oh," she says. "Was he scared on the way over?" She looks at my dad and then at me.

"A little cat-er-walling," my dad says. "Not too much."

Spot made some very strange noises on the way over—deep noises, nothing like the little meow he's making now. I wonder if that's what "cat-er-walling" means.

"He's a dog-cat," I say again.

"I've heard," Kathy says.

"He plays fetch," I say proudly.

"I know," she says.

"I'm always up for a game of fetch," Max says.

My dad looks around the house. "Looks good," he says. "I like what you did with the kitchen."

"Thanks," Max says.

My dad glances at the sliding glass door, out

to the backyard at the lime tree, and his face goes serious. "Sorry about Bruno," my dad says.

"I'm sorry too," I say.

"He was a great dog," Kathy says.

"The best dog," Max says, and I'm not sure but I think his eyes might be welling up, and I decide right then and there that if I can't keep Spot, then Kathy and Max and Cameron and Eddie are the perfect people to take over.

"I've always wanted a cat too," Eddie says.

"Cats can live more than twenty years," I say.

And my dad and Kathy and Max all smile. Max shakes my dad's hand again and tells him he stayed to say hello and meet the famous Spot, but he has to head into the office for a few hours.

"Do you want to see our garden, Abigail Iris?" Kathy asks me.

I nod and follow her out past the lime tree, and I think about Bruno. Kathy takes me to a very sunny corner of the yard where she introduces me to the plants she's growing— green peppers, cherry tomatoes, celery, and watermelon. The watermelons are green and the size of tennis balls.

"They're just babies," she says.

"Like Spot," I say. "And my Only friend Rebecca's new little brother, Stephen. He's still so new he's all squirmy."

"I remember when your brothers were brand new like that," Kathy says.

This is very hard to imagine, tiny little Eddie and Cameron wearing diapers and squirming around on Kathy's shoulder.

"You know, I could use some regular help with weeding," she says. "The boys aren't particularly interested, but you look like you have a green thumb, Abigail Iris."

"I do?" I say. No one's ever told me that before.

"You do," Kathy says.

I think about how it's too bad I never got around to coming over here before now.

"What if you come help me weed once or twice a week and visit Spot at the same time?" Kathy asks.

"I think that sounds like a very good idea," I say, imagining visiting Spot and bringing home vegetables to my mother that are even more just-fresh-picked than the fresh-picked ones at the farmers' market. Even though I prefer to play four square and tetherball than volunteer to weed the Learning Garden at Bayside Elementary at lunchtime, I really do want to weed this garden with Kathy. To show I know what I'm doing, I bend down right away and pull up a big, splotchy weed and hand it to her as if it's a present.

She brushes it off and says, "Isn't it amazing the way celery grows? I'll use this in my tuna salad tomorrow. Thank you."

"Time to go, Abigail Iris," my father shouts from the sliding door.

I'm glad to see Spot back in his carrier and the carrier in my father's hand. I decide I very much like Cameron and Eddie's mother, who doesn't seem at all mad at me for not knowing the difference between a weed and celery, but I'm still not ready to leave Spot here just yet.

"See you soon!" Kathy says as she walks us to the front door. Eddie is staying behind at his other house, and he's standing on the front stoop with Kathy, waving.

"That is definitely the house I most prefer for Spot if he has to move instead of Victoria," I say to Old Man Cheeto as we drive off, Spot meowing in what I decide must be agreement from his carrier in the backseat.

Chapter 13

On his exact one-month birthday, Stephen Jeremy gets to come to school with Martha to pick up Rebecca. Genevieve, Cynthia, and I are all very excited, waiting for him by the curb. Even though Rebecca lives exactly one-half mile away, according to Cynthia, who has excellent math skills and likes to measure distances, Martha and Stephen are walking, not driving, to get us. It turns out my no-longer-Only friend's little brother hates the car almost as much as Spot does.

We're all going home with Rebecca and staying until five p.m. Rebecca, who, in my mother's opinion, has turned into a very good little planner, called up every one of us last night to set this up.

Billy Doil, as usual, is hanging around with us after school. "What's going on?" he says.

"Can't you see we're waiting for our ride home?" Genevieve says.

"Is your brother picking everyone up today, Abigail Iris?" Billy Doil says to me.

"Not today," I say. "We're walking home with Rebecca's new baby."

"Cool," Billy Doil says.

"They're late, huh?" he adds a minute later.

"Obviously," Genevieve says, and I think it's a good thing that Rebecca, not Genevieve, has the new brother she'll have to be very patient with.

I am surprised when Martha finally shows up, and I don't see her fancy new stroller anywhere. She has Jazzy with her, and he starts pulling on his leash extra hard when he sees Rebecca.

"Jazzy, my Jazzy," Rebecca says, bending down to rub him under his chin.

I wonder if Martha forgot the baby at

home because he was so young she hadn't gotten into the habit of him yet. But then I see he's plastered to the front of her, strapped in some kind of carrier. He's still so tiny, the top of his head barely sticks out of the top.

"Calm down, Jazzy," Martha says. "It's not as easy as it looks," she adds, and I nod and smile even though I'm not sure what she's talking about.

"How come Stephen Jeremy isn't in his fancy new stroller?" I ask.

"Oh, he likes being next to his mama," she says. "Did you know little babies like to feel a beating heart? It relaxes them."

"I didn't know that," I say very seriously, because Martha tells me this information in a way that makes it sound important. She sounds almost exactly the way Mrs. Aaronson does when something she tells us will be on a chapter test later.

"I can walk with you all partway if you want, Abigail Iris," Billy Doil says. "You go right by my street."

"Cool," I say, and then Genevieve elbows me hard in the side. "Whatever," I say.

Billy Doil finds a rock to kick and knocks it back and forth between his feet as he walks, like it's a soccer ball, and I am reminded that even if he can be annoying, he's one of the third graders you hope to get on your team when you have soccer in PE class.

While Billy Doil kicks his rock, Rebecca, Genevieve, Cynthia, and I take turns walking Jazzy. He stops every few feet and sniffs at spots of grass he finds particularly appealing. Martha bounces up and down with the baby a little whenever we stop with Jazzy.

"Stephen likes constant motion," Martha tells us when Cynthia asks her why she's bouncing.

I'm thinking this baby has a lot of opinions for someone who's only one month old. I'm thinking that my once-Only friend Rebecca is in bigger trouble than I thought.

"'Bye, ladies," Billy Doil says, saluting a little at us when he gets to his corner. "See you tomorrow, Abigail Iris," he says to me especially.

Genevieve sighs heavily. "Boys," she says.

Stephen Jeremy starts crying even though Martha is doing an excellent job of bouncing him up and down just the way he likes her to.

"Yeah, boys," Rebecca says, who has stopped with Jazzy again.

Rebecca is grouchy at the moment, so I take her hand and swing her arm a little to cheer her up, and then we both skip on ahead in front of everyone just enough to keep ourselves in a good mood.

"I should be sad but I'm not," I tell Rebecca as we skip.

"Why, Abigail Iris?" Rebecca asks me.

"Why what?"

"Why should you be sad?"

"Because tomorrow is moving day for Spot," I tell her.

"Oh," Rebecca says, skipping a little slower now. "Then why aren't you sad?"

"Because Spot's tired of living in my parents' bedroom, and he'll still be in the family, and because his new house is very cozy and friendly, and I'm going to visit him all the time when I help Eddie and Cameron's mom weed her garden."

Rebecca and I have stopped our skipping now and are waiting at the corner for the rest of them to catch up because we aren't allowed to cross the street by ourselves.

"Well, maybe I'm a little sad," I say, feeling that way all at once. "But it's not the kind of sad like when your dog dies," I say, thinking of Bruno.

Rebecca nods and gives me what my mother would call a brave little smile, and I know that she understands what I'm talking about.

"We're both not Onlies together," I say. I pause and think for a minute. "It's not always so bad not being an Only," I tell her, and I think of some of the good things like how the house never feels empty and there's always someone to talk to or peel potatoes with. "Just wait a few years," I say. "You guys can share cheesy popcorn from the farmers' market."

"Stephen Jeremy doesn't even have teeth yet," Rebecca says.

"But he will," I say. "Kids grow up too fast," I tell her, thinking about what Old Man Cheeto says every year on my birthday.

Everyone's caught up with us now, so Rebecca and I hold hands and skip with gusto across the street.

୬

At Rebecca's house, we all bounce on her trampoline in the backyard while Martha feeds the baby. I'm used to having a snack right away after school, but I don't say anything because I am trying to be a good guest. Still, my stomach is making grumbling noises while I jump. Everyone is laughing so hard, I don't think anyone can hear my stomach.

"Is anyone ready for a snack?" Martha finally calls out to us.

"I am!" I shout, forgetting all about my good

manners. I'm the first one to slide off the trampoline and seat myself at the kitchen table.

Martha is opening the refrigerator and getting out cheese sticks and carrot sticks, and she's pouring us glasses of lemonade with real slices of lemon in it.

"This is a delicious after-school snack," I say, hoping that maybe she's got a little something hidden in there for dessert for us too, if we have excellent appetites and manners.

Martha leans over the kitchen table and helps herself to a carrot stick. "The baby's finally asleep," she says, although none of us have asked her where he is. "What do you girls say we celebrate?" Martha pulls a carton of ice cream out of the freezer and places it on the table next to the cheese sticks. She hands each of us a soup spoon. "Who likes chocolate chip cookie dough?" she asks.

"Dig in, girls, dig in," Rebecca says. Her old silly self again, Rebecca takes the first big spoonful.

And then we all dig in too.

When Eddie picks me up from Rebecca's house, I hop in the backseat and notice right away that he has a new haircut with flat bangs that cut across his forehead. "What's up with your hair?" I ask.

"Do you think Molly will like it?" Eddie says.

"Well," I say.

"What?" he says.

I see Eddie's worried face looking at me in the rearview mirror. "I'm sure she will," I say. "I much prefer it this new way myself." This is what my father, Old Man Cheeto, would call a not-really-a-lie. Every time we eat dinner at my grandmother's house in San Diego, he reminds me about these not-really-a-lies in the car on the way down. "Just tell her you enjoyed the gefilte fish, Abigail Iris," he tells me. "Then push it under your lettuce."

"Did you have fun at Rebecca's?" he asks.

I nod my head. "Do you know when you have a new baby in your family, you get to eat ice cream right out of the container?" I tell him.

"Is that right?" he says.

"Absolutely," I say.

"Abigail Iris, Cameron and I have been talking, and we decided Spot will definitely still be your cat, too," Eddie says, "even though he'll live with us."

"Really?" I say.

"Absolutely," he says. "How could he not be?"

I think about this question and how it's not really a question at all. Spot belongs to my whole family.

"Are you ready for his big move?" Eddie asks me.

I think about this for a minute. I think about Rebecca and Stephen Jeremy and how she wasn't really ready for him, but now he's here and we're all starting to get used to him, maybe even like him. And how maybe I'll get used to Spot living at my brothers' other house but still being my cat, too.

"Yes and no," I say. "But mostly yes." And this is not a not-really-a-lie. I am mostly ready. I lean over and rub the top of my brother's new hairdo to see what it feels like. It's softer than I thought it would be, and rubbing it feels lucky. "Yes I am," I say. "Let's get Spot ready for his big move," I tell him.

Chapter 14

Before Spot moves to his new house, I decide that I need to spend some alone time with him to explain things and say my special good-bye, which isn't quite good-bye because he'll still be in the family and I'll still get to see his cute face when I help Eddie and Cameron's other mom with the garden.

It's early morning, before breakfast, and I'm on my parents' bed, which isn't even made yet. Spot is playing our version of hide-and-seek, which means that he nudges himself under the covers and thinks he's hiding from me, but he's actually a little lump that is very visible.

"Where's Spot?" I say into the air, although

I know exactly where he is. "Where's Spot?" I say again, and he pokes his face out, the sheet draping his head and flattening his ears.

I pat my lap and Spot comes over and sits down. He's purring and purring and I'm telling him all the things I'm going to miss about seeing him on a daily basis.

"Your little motor is only one of the things I'll miss about you," I say. And he purrs even louder.

I tell him that I'll miss waking up and rushing into my parents' room to say good morning.

I'll miss feeding him and giving him treats in the late afternoon.

I'll miss playing fetch with him.

I'll miss his paws and tail and pink nose.

I'll miss his soft belly.

I'll especially miss hide-and-seek.

Still, I must admit that having three guardians is even better than having one or two, and then I assure him that I'll visit him regularly and that he'll always be *my* Spot.

Because my mom is already worried about me being sad, she decides that she'll be the one to pack up Spot's things. She's standing at the bedroom door, with one foot inside to block Spot, who's jumped from my lap and is very interested in what's happening in the living room. My dad's watching the television and talking to the newscaster, who's apparently very irritating. Spot's poking his head around my mom's slipper, trying to figure out a path, and he's just about figured out his escape, when she steps into the bedroom and closes the door behind her.

"Let me get in here, Abigail Iris. I want to make the bed and pack up the rest of Spot's things."

"I'll help," I say, standing up.

"You can help me with the bed," she says.

"And then I'll help you pack Spot's toys."

"No," she says gently.

"No?"

"I don't even want you to watch, Abigail Iris," she says.

"I want to help," I say.

"Not your job," she tells me, tightening her robe at the waist.

And even though I insist that I'm fine, she shoos me away. "Your dad's going to make pancakes in a few minutes. You can help him in the kitchen."

"Okay," I say.

"You can heat up the syrup," she says.

༃

Molly comes over to join us for breakfast, and she's brought a new toy for Spot—a cushy ball with a bell inside of it. Before we eat, she follows me into my parents' bedroom to see Spot and bring him his toy. Because his other toys are all packed up now, he's probably very grateful to have a new one. Molly tosses the ball to the floor and Spot bats it under the bed and chases it. Then he bats it into the corner and chases it, and then he bats it back under the bed. He does this again and again and again.

Finally, when he's all tired out, he flops down in front of the door and rests.

After Spot's rested a few minutes, he looks up at the door and stands up on his hind legs, stretching and swatting at the doorknob.

"He needs more space," Molly says. And then she looks at me. "I mean, I'm sure he loves you and is happy to live here, but he wants out, huh?"

"Yeah," I say.

"I'm sure he'll miss you," she says.

"He'll like living at Eddie and Cameron's house. And I'll still get to see him all the time," I say.

"You're really mature for your age, Abigail Iris," she says. "I knew it the first time I met you."

"Well, thank you very much," I say, trying to sound even more mature than I apparently am.

Then Molly tells me all about a bird she rescued when she was my age—a sparrow named Sam, who one day flew out of the living room window and never came back. "I cried and cried," she says. "I couldn't believe he wanted to live anywhere but with our family."

"He was mostly in a cage, right?" I say.

"Yep," she says.

"I understand why he left," I say.

She sighs. She nods. "I do too," she says, "finally, but it didn't dawn on me for a long time. One day it just hit me: of course, he didn't like being cooped up."

"Spot will be happier when he has a whole house to explore," I say, sounding like my mom.

"That's what I mean about mature, Abigail Iris. You understand and you don't even have to wait years and years for it to dawn on you."

৵

After a big breakfast of my dad's amazing pancakes, Victoria gives Spot a special hug and kiss good-bye, not even worrying about her allergies. I decide right then and there that Victoria needs a hug too, and I'm just the one to do it.

"I would just like to say that I forgive you, Victoria," I say, after I pull away.

"You *forgive* me?" Victoria says.

"Yes. Yes, I do," I say. "I know you really can't help taking after Grandma."

"That's very big of you," Old Man Cheeto says.

"Why does she get to forgive me for something that isn't my fault?" Victoria says.

"I think what Abigail Iris means is she doesn't blame you," my mother says.

I much prefer my way of saying it. But I don't feel like arguing, so I say, "That must be what I mean." Then I give Victoria one more quick hug good-bye.

ॐ

Eddie, Molly, and I are in the car taking Spot to his new home. Eddie's driving and I'm sitting in the back with Spot's carrier on my lap. This time, he's not making those strange noises, but he's still poking his nose out and trying to see what's up.

"Tell Abigail Iris about the new pet-supply place," Eddie says.

"They opened up the best new store," Molly says. "And it's right next door to my bookstore." She pulls on her seat belt at the neck and turns around to face me.

"They've got great stuff," Eddie says, nodding.

"I'm going to bring Spot toys and treats,"

she says. "And sometimes I can even stop by and pick you up before dropping them off, Abigail Iris."

"Really?" I say, excited.

"Yep," she says. "I promise."

"You're a good person," I say.

"How sweet," she says. "So mature," she tells Eddie.

I push a crunchy tuna treat into Spot's cage and nod in agreement.

ॐ

When we pull into the driveway, I see Eddie moving a piece of hair away from his eyes and remember his new haircut. "Doesn't Eddie's hair look good?" I say.

"It looks great," Molly says, smiling.

"Oh, we're so glad you like it," I say, looking at Eddie, who's giving me a don't-say-anything-else look in the rearview mirror.

"*We* are?" Molly smiles, nudging Eddie in the ribs.

"Let's get Spot moved in," he says, changing

the subject and turning off the car. "It's time to show him his new digs."

"He's been here before," I remind him.

"I know, I know," Eddie says, opening his door and stepping out. "I'm just saying."

Molly steps outside too.

And I don't even unlock my door.

I sit and sit.

I hold Spot's carrier tightly.

I wait until Eddie comes over and unlocks the door for me, until he takes the carrier from my lap, until Molly offers me her hand. "Come on," she says sweetly. "Let's go."

I take a deep breath.

I step out of the car, take Molly's hand, and follow the three of them up the walkway and into the house.

Chapter 15

"Welcome, welcome, welcome," Kathy says, opening the front door. That's one welcome for each one of us, and I think that Kathy is a very fair person.

"And a very special welcome to you, Spot." Kathy puts her nose right up to the carrier. Then she takes it from Eddie, and we follow her into the house. Kathy places the carrier down gently, smack in the middle of their living room coffee table, right on top of a very important-looking art book. Then she opens the little door.

Spot stands at the doorway and peers out at her.

"Sometimes he's a little shy," I say.

"Oh, of course," Kathy says. "What am I thinking?" She backs away a few feet, and we all watch as Spot walks out onto the coffee table and looks around at his new living room.

"You're a good person, Kathy," I say.

"Thank you, Abigail Iris," she says.

"Welcome to your new home," Eddie says.

I'm watching Spot tiptoe around now, but I'm also watching Molly squeeze Eddie's hand a little. "He's going to like it here," I say, and I 100 percent mean it. It's going to be sad not to be able to visit Spot in my parents' bedroom, but I'm happy Spot has a whole house to explore without worrying about making anyone sneeze. I take the toy Molly got for him, the cushy ball with the little bell inside it, out of my pocket. I throw it all the way across the living room, and Spot pounces after it.

When Cameron and his other dad come in the front door carrying grocery bags, Spot is playing fetch with his new toy, taking turns delivering it to each one of us.

"Unbelievable," Max says.

"I told you," Cameron says.

"Spot is one very special cat," I say.

"And you're one very special girl," Max says, "to let him live here with us."

"Being stuck in a bedroom all day is no life for a cat," I say.

"Come on out back with me for a minute," Kathy says.

Even though I visited Kathy's garden just a little over a week ago, it looks different. For one thing, instead of being hard little green balls, some of the tomatoes are actually red and softer-looking now. Kathy hands me a plastic bowl and tells me to pick whatever I want to take home to my mother.

We bend down together and decide what's ripe.

I take a head of flouncy-looking red lettuce.

I take three perfectly red tomatoes.

I pull up a stalk of celery, and this time I know it's not a weed.

"Take some rosemary, too," Kathy says,

pulling me off a bunch. "Doesn't it smell good?"

"Delightful," I say, inhaling deeply. "I will help you weed twice a week forever," I say.

We walk back inside the house, and I see everyone is sitting in the living room now, looking at something Cameron is holding. I look, too, and I see Spot curled up on Cameron's chest. Spot's eyes are closed. When I get close enough I can hear his special purr sound.

"He's all worn out from playing fetch," Cameron says.

"He's just a baby, and babies nap a lot," I say. Then I think of Henry nearly falling asleep at the lunch benches with us, and I add, "If you're lucky."

My arms are full with my big plastic bowl, overflowing with vegetables. I put it down for a minute so my hands are free to pet Spot good-bye before Eddie and Molly drive me home.

"I'll visit you all the time," I whisper to Spot

in his soft little ear. "Look, you're already happy here," I tell him.

Molly picks up my bowl of vegetables and Eddie takes my hand as we walk to his car. He swings my arm back and forth a little with his, and I let go and stand on my tiptoes to

rub the top of his new haircut before we get in his car. "You look different, but I'm getting used to it," I say.

"Very handsome," Molly says.

I buckle myself in the middle of the back-seat, my bowl of vegetables next to me where Spot's carrier used to be, and I lean forward so my head is right between Molly's and Eddie's. "Home, James," I say.

"Who's James?" Molly says.

"I don't know," I say. "It's just something we say sometimes in my family," I tell her. "Victoria made it up."

When Eddie stays stopped at a light after it turns green, I say, "How green does green have to be?"

"Let me guess," Molly says. "That's something else you say in your family."

And then Eddie and Molly start talking about other things that are special in our families, how our dad is called Old Man Cheeto and how her big sister calls her college roommate Superwoman. Soon the car is filled with talking and laughing and the smell of the special rosemary that Kathy grows in her garden.

I, Abigail Iris, have an Only best friend who is an Only no more. I finally got a pet for my half birthday. Even though he can't live in my house, Spot is still my special kitty, and I will visit him all the time. And I am on the way home to surprise my mother with so many fresh vegetables, she might just have to catch her breath when she sees me.

Lisa Glatt is the author of the Abigail Iris series, as well as *A Girl Becomes a Comma Like That* and *The Apple's Bruise*. She lives in California with her husband and their two cats. www.lisaglatt.com

Suzanne Greenberg is the author of the Abigail Iris series, as well as *Speed-Walk and Other Stories*, and the coauthor of *Everyday Creative Writing*. She lives in California with her husband and their three children. www.suzannegreenberg.com

Joy Allen has illustrated more than thirty books, including the Abigail Iris series and the popular American Girl: Hopscotch Hill School series. She lives in California. www.joyallenillustration.com

Abigail Iris
sure is one of a kind.

Don't miss

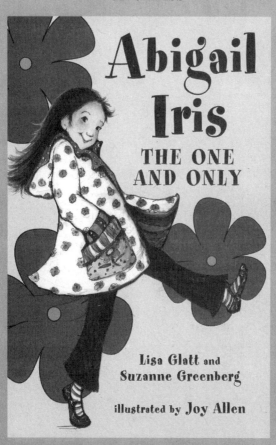

Abigail
Iris
THE ONE
AND ONLY

Lisa Glatt and
Suzanne Greenberg

illustrated by Joy Allen

Walker & Company